"What the hell's going on?" Jordan demanded.

Molly didn't answer him. Instead, she poured her soon-to-be ex-husband a stiff drink.

"What's that for?" he asked, frowning.

"You might want to sit down."

Molly had thought she could do this unemotionally, but she was wrong. She was shaking like meadow grass stirred by high winds.

"What's gotten into you?" Jordan insisted. "I realize this divorce thing is more wrenching than either of us expected, but—"

"Oh, honestly, Jordan," Molly said impatiently, "don't be so obtuse. We made love, remember?"

"Yeah, but why bring it up now?"

As soon as the words left his lips, Jordan made the connection. His eyes linked with hers. And he reached for his tumbler and drank it down.

"You're...you're pregnant...."

Dear Reader,

Welcome to Silhouette Special Edition...welcome to romance.

The hot month of July starts off with a sizzling event! Debbie Macomber's fiftieth book, *Baby Blessed,* is our THAT SPECIAL WOMAN! for July. This emotional, heartwarming book in which the promise of a new life reunites a husband and wife is not to be missed!

Christine Rimmer's series THE JONES GANG continues in *Sweetbriar Summit* with sexy Patrick Jones, the second of the rapscallion Jones brothers you'll meet. You'll want to be around when the Jones boys bring their own special brand of trouble to town!

Also this month, look for books by some of your favorite authors: Celeste Hamilton presents us with an emotional tale in *Which Way Is Home?* and Susan Mallery has a *Cowboy Daddy* waiting to find a family. July also offers *Unpredictable* by Patt Bucheister, and *Homeward Bound* by Sierra Rydell, her follow-up to *On Middle Ground.* A veritable light show of July fireworks!

I hope you enjoy this book, and all of the stories to come!

Sincerely,

Tara Gavin
Senior Editor

Please address questions and book requests to:
Silhouette Reader Service
U.S.: 3010 Walden Ave., P.O. Box 1325, Buffalo, NY 14269
Canadian: P.O. Box 609, Fort Erie, Ont. L2A 5X3

DEBBIE MACOMBER

BABY BLESSED

Silhouette®

SPECIAL EDITION®

Published by Silhouette Books
America's Publisher of Contemporary Romance

For
Cindy DeBerry, a steadfast friend through the years

 SILHOUETTE BOOKS

ISBN 0-373-09895-2

BABY BLESSED

Copyright © 1994 by Debbie Macomber

Printed in U.S.A.

Books by Debbie Macomber

DEBBIE MACOMBER

hails from the state of Washington. As a busy wife and mother of four, she strives to keep her family healthy and happy. As the prolific author of dozens of best-selling romance novels, she strives to keep her readers happy with each new book she writes.

A Note from the Author

Dear Reader,

It all started in the late 1970s, when I was a housewife and mother with a king-size dream. I wanted to write romance novels. In between car pools, soccer games and music lessons, I began putting my imagination to work on a rented typewriter at our kitchen table.

Fifty books and sixteen years later, much has changed. My children have grown, that old upright typewriter's been replaced by a state-of-the-art computer that talks back to me and the kitchen table's become an office, with a personal assistant, files, a fax and four phone lines!

I'm grateful to Silhouette for giving me the opportunity to live out my dream. My life changed the day Mary Clare Kersten phoned to say she'd like to make an offer on my book. Fourteen months later, *Starlight* was on the shelves, and my career was born.

Baby Blessed is a special book that comes straight from my heart. I hope Molly and Jordan's story touches yours. Be sure and take a good look at the cover models. That beautiful woman is my daughter, Jody, and that handsome young man is my son Ted. I'm exceptionally proud of them both. Putting them on the cover is Silhouette's gift to me.

If there was one thing I could say to each of you, it's to dream big dreams. Don't stuff them into the future with justifications and excuses. Don't be afraid. Who knows where they might take you.

As always, I'm delighted to hear from my readers. You can reach me at P.O. Box 1458, Port Orchard, WA 98366.

Debbie Macomber

Chapter One

"All right, I'll play your little game," Jordan Larabee said between gritted teeth as he paced the thick carpet in front of Ian Houghton's shiny mahogany desk. "Just where the hell is she?"

"I presume you mean Molly?"

Ian could be a real smartass when he wanted to be, and apparently he'd fine-tuned it into an art form since their last meeting.

"I might remind you Molly is *your* wife."

"She's your daughter," Jordan shot back. "It was you she went to when she left me."

Ian relaxed against the high-back leather chair, seeming to enjoy himself. An insolent half smile curled up the edges of his mouth. "It was my understanding Molly's leaving was a mutual decision."

Jordan snickered. "By the time she moved out there wasn't anything mutual between us. We hadn't spoken in days." The communication between them had died with their six-month-old son. The autumn morning they'd lowered Jeff's tiny casket into the ground, they'd buried their marriage, as well. For eight months afterward, they'd struggled to hold their lives together. But the grief and the guilt had eaten away until there was nothing left but an empty shell, and eventually that had crumbled and scattered like dust.

Ian stood, looking older than Jordan remembered. He walked over to the window and gazed out as if the view were mesmerizing. "Why now?"

"It's been three years," Jordan reminded him.

"I'm well aware of how long it's been," Ian murmured, clenching his hands behind his back.

"It's time I got on with my life," Jordan said coolly. "I want a divorce."

"A divorce," Ian repeated, and it seemed his shoulders sagged under the weight of the word.

"Don't tell me this comes as a shock. I should have filed years ago." Jordan paced the room with ill patience, the anger simmering just below the surface until it felt like a geyser about to erupt. His annoyance was unreasonable, Jordan realized, and directed more at himself than his father-in-law. He'd delayed this confrontation for longer than he should have, dreading it. The divorce papers were tucked away in his briefcase. All he sought was Molly's signature. After three years, he didn't anticipate Molly's objection. Actually he was surprised she hadn't taken the action herself.

Ian moved away from the window and glanced toward the framed picture on his desk. Jordan knew it was one taken of him and Molly shortly after Jeff had been born. He remembered it well. He was standing behind Molly, who held Jeff in her arms; his hand was braced on Molly's shoulder and the two of them were gazing down with wonderment and love on this young life they'd produced. Little did they know that their joy would soon turn into the deepest grief they'd ever experience.

"I'd always hoped you two would patch things up," Ian said, his words tinged with sadness.

Jordan pressed his lips together and buried his hands deep inside his pants pockets. A reconciliation might have worked earlier, but it was impossible now; the sooner Ian accepted that, the better. "I've met someone else."

Ian nodded. "I guessed as much. You can't blame an old man for wishing."

"Where's Molly?" Jordan wasn't enjoying this cat-and-mouse game any more than Ian. The time had come to cut to the chase.

"Manukua," Ian told him.

Jordan's head snapped up. "Africa?"

Ian nodded. "She's doing volunteer work with some church group. The country's desperately in need of anyone with medical experience, and working there has seemed to help her."

Jordan splayed his fingers through his hair. "How long has she been there?"

"Over two years now."

"Two years?" Jordan felt as if he'd taken a blow to the abdomen and slumped into a nearby chair. It was just like Molly to do something impulsive. Manukua had been in the news almost nightly, with accounts of rebel unrest, drought, disease and God only knew what else.

"I've done everything I know how to convince her to come home," Ian said, sitting back down himself, "but she won't listen to me."

"What's the matter with her?" Jordan demanded.

"The same thing as you, I suspect," Ian said without rancor. "You buried yourself in your work, and she's dedicated herself to saving the world."

"Any fool would know Manukua's not safe," Jordan protested heatedly, furious with his soon-to-be ex-wife.

Ian nodded, agreeing with him. "She claims otherwise. Apparently she's working in a hospital in Makua, the capital, for two weeks out of the month. Then she commutes into the backcountry to a medical compound for another two weeks."

"Is she crazy, traveling outside of the city?" Jordan demanded. He wished Molly was there so he could strangle her himself. He was on his feet again, but didn't remember standing. "The woman should have her head examined."

"I couldn't agree with you more. Something's got to be done." He grinned and reached for a Cuban cigar. "As far as I'm concerned, you're the man for it."

"Me? What the hell can I do?" Jordan asked, although he was fairly certain he already knew the answer.

For the first time Jordan read a genuine smile in the older man's eyes. "What can you do?" Ian repeated meaningfully. "Why, Jordan, you can go get her yourself."

It was the evenings that Molly loved best, when the compound slept and the night slipped in—silent, cool and welcome. She sat outside on the veranda and drank in the sounds, allowing them to soothe her exhausted body and spirit. The news from headquarters in Makua had arrived earlier that evening and it hadn't been good. It never was. Each report, no matter where or when she was in the backcountry, seemed filled with dire warnings and evil threats. That evening's communication had been no different, with a lengthy account of political unrest in the capital city and the threat of a rebel attack. Headquarters asked that she and Dr. Morton be prepared to evacuate at a moment's notice. The identical message came through on a regular basis and had long since lost its urgency. At the end of the week they'd return to Makua the same way they did every month.

The black stillness of the night was filled with gentle sounds from the water hole just outside the compound walls. The savanna was a refuge for the dwindling animal population. The drought had taken a dramatic toll on wildlife, just as it had on the natives.

Just a week earlier Molly had witnessed a small herd of elephants tramping across the dry plain, stirring up a haze of red dust. They were moving, looking for a more abundant water supply, Molly guessed.

A hyena yipped in the night, and she smiled softly to herself. Additional sounds drifted toward her as the antelope and other beasts made their way to the water's waning edge to cool their thirst. Over time and with patience, Molly had become adept at identifying each species. She'd discovered, contrary to popular belief, that lions didn't roar so much as cough. She'd hear the king of beasts and then the night would go quiet as his intended prey silently slipped away from the water's edge.

Leaning back in the white wicker chair, she stretched her arms high above her head and stared into the heavens. The sky was illuminated with an incredible display of stars, but she would have sold her inheritance for the sight of a water-fat rain cloud.

Unfortunately the sky was disgustingly clear. Molly couldn't look into the night without experiencing a twinge of sadness. Somewhere in a world far removed from what was her life now remained the husband she'd abandoned and the son she'd buried.

She tried not to think about either, because doing so produced a dull, throbbing pain. And pain was something she'd spent the past three years running away from, until she was breathless and emotionally exhausted from the effort. The gold wedding band on her finger felt like an accusation. She wasn't even sure why she continued to wear it. Habit, she suspected, and to ward off any who thought she might be interested in romance. She wasn't.

Familiar footsteps sounded behind her.

"Good evening," Molly greeted her associate. Dr. Richard Morton was well past the age of retirement, short, bald and lovable, but he didn't know how to stop working, not when the need remained so great. Molly, who was slender as a reed, stood nearly a head taller. With her short blond hair and deep blue eyes, she caused something of a sensation with the black African children.

"Why aren't you asleep?" Molly asked her friend. By all rights they should both have fallen into bed exhausted.

"I haven't figured that out myself," the physician said, settling into the chair next to her. "Something's in the air."

"Oh?"

"I've got a feeling about this last message from Makua."

"You think we should leave?" Richard couldn't have surprised her more. Her companion had never revealed any signs of being anxious for their safety in the past, even when the radio messages had sounded far more urgent.

Richard shrugged and wiped a hand down his face. "I don't know, but something tells me this time is different."

This past week had been hectic with an outbreak of influenza, and they'd both been working grueling hours, often as many as eighteen a day.

"You're overly tired," Molly suggested, searching for a plausible excuse for his qualms.

"We both are," Richard murmured and gently patted her hand. "Go to bed and we'll talk about this some more in the morning."

Molly followed his advice, taking a few extra moments to stroll through the pediatric ward. The nurse on duty smiled when she saw who it was. The walk through the children's ward had become something of a ritual for her.

Silently moving between cribs, Molly stopped to check if each child was breathing. This was the legacy SIDS had given her. It was as though she anticipated that terrible scene replaying itself over again with another child in another time and place. The fear never left her. The fear of losing another child had taken up residence in the deepest roots of her heart.

Once she was assured all was well, Molly made her way into her own tiny room, not bothering to turn on the light. She undressed and slipped between the cool sheets, closed her eyes and dreamed of what her life would have been like if Jeff had lived.

"I'm sorry I'm late," Jordan said, kissing Lesley's cheek before pulling out the chair and sitting down at the table across from her. Each time Jordan was with the accomplished architect he was struck by her charm and beauty. "How long did I keep you waiting this time?" he asked as he unfolded the pink linen napkin and placed it on his lap.

"Only a few moments."

He was a full fifteen minutes late, and knowing Lesley she'd arrived five minutes early, yet she didn't complain. This was one of the things he liked best about her. She understood his preoccupation with work, because she was often deeply involved in a project herself.

Jordan reached for the menu, scanned the contents and quickly made his choice, setting it aside.

"Don't keep me in suspense," Lesley said. "Tell me how the meeting with Ian went."

Jordan shrugged, not sure he wanted to talk about Molly or Ian just yet. He found it awkward to be discussing his wife with the woman he intended to marry. There'd been a time when he'd hoped he and Molly might be able to salvage their marriage. But as the weeks and months slipped past and neither of them seemed inclined to breach the silence, Jordan lost hope for a reconciliation.

"Everything went fine," he said, reaching for the wine list, studying the different choices.

"You don't want to talk about it, do you?" Lesley said after a moment.

"Not particularly."

"All right...I can understand that," she said, and although he could read the disappointment in her voice he knew she wouldn't pursue the issue further. This was something else he appreciated about Lesley. He'd known her for years and couldn't remember her so much as raising her voice, even once.

In the past year they'd started working together on a large construction project on Chicago's east side. She was the architect and he was the builder. Heaven knew he wasn't looking for another relationship. Falling in love a second time held no appeal.

Ian was right when he claimed Jordan had buried himself in his work after Jeff's death. He went from one project to the next with barely a breath in between. He didn't know what would happen if he ever stopped—he didn't want to know.

"I realize this is difficult for you," Lesley said in that soft, sultry voice of hers. "But you must know what an awkward position this puts me in. I can't continue to date a married man."

"I do understand."

"Nor do I want to force you into a divorce when it's something you may not want."

Jordan frowned. This ground was all too familiar, and he wasn't thrilled to be traipsing over the same worn path. "The marriage is dead." If he'd said it once, he'd said it a hundred times.

"You told me that in the beginning," Lesley reminded him, "but we've been seeing each other steadily for six months and in all that time you didn't once mention divorcing Molly." This sounded faintly like an accusation.

"I should have filed years ago."

"But you didn't."

Jordan didn't need Lesley to tell him that.

"Do you know why?" she pressed. Generally she was willing to let sleeping dogs lie, but not this evening.

"I was too busy," he said, a bit more heatedly than he intended. "Besides, I assumed Molly would see to it."

"She didn't file for a divorce, either, you'll notice," Lesley felt obliged to point out to him. "Have you stopped to consider that?"

He nodded, and motioned for a waiter, who promptly appeared and took their order. Jordan asked for a bottle of chardonnay and for the next five or so minutes he was preoccupied with the opening and tasting of the wine. Jordan hoped Lesley would drop the subject of Molly and the divorce, but he doubted she would. Her pretty brown eyes were aimed at him with the same gentle persuasion he'd witnessed the night she'd first announced she couldn't continue to date a married man. Rather than lose her, he'd agreed to start the divorce proceedings.

"You're still in love with her, aren't you?" Lesley pressed in that delicate way of hers. She was rarely angry at him, unlike Molly who took delight in igniting his ire. Lesley was subtle and concerned. Whatever her methods, they worked wonders on him.

"It's perfectly understandable, you realize," Lesley continued.

"To love Molly?" He couldn't believe she was suggesting such a thing.

"Yes. What happened to the two of you is tragic."

A pain tightened in his chest. "She blamed herself," he whispered, his hand gripping the wineglass with unnecessary force. "With all her medical training she seemed to think there was something she could have done to save him.''

He'd argued with her until he had no voice left. It hadn't helped matters that he'd left the house when she and Jeff were still asleep. Apparently Jeff had stirred and cried out, but it was early yet and, thinking she'd get a few more moments sleep, Molly had ignored the lone cry. It was the last sound their son had ever made. Molly had woken an hour later to discover Jeff dead.

Jordan looked at Lesley and blinked, wondering if what she suggested was true. Did he still love Molly? He'd never faulted her for what happened to Jeff, but she'd readily accepted the blame herself, despite everything he said and did.

But did he love Molly? Jordan asked himself a second time. He didn't know. So much of what he felt toward her was tangled up in his feelings for his son. He'd loved Jeff more than he thought it was possible for a man to love his child. He'd grieved, in his own way, until he had nearly killed himself, working all hours of the day and night. In some way he suspected he had died. Part of him had departed with his son.

If Jordan had learned anything from his limited experience as a father, it was that he would never be vulnerable to this kind of pain again. This was Lesley's great appeal. She didn't want children, either. They were perfect for each other.

''I don't mean to pressure you with these uncomfortable questions,'' Lesley continued in soft, caring tones.

''You're not,'' Jordan said. The loss of his son wasn't a subject he'd ever feel comfortable sharing. But if he was going to join his life with Lesley's, Jeff was a topic they needed to talk about.

The waiter delivered their salads, and Lesley, who sensed his mood perfectly, left Jordan alone with his thoughts.

At some point this evening he'd need to tell Lesley he was going to Manukua after Molly. He didn't relish the task.

He'd like to wring Molly's pretty neck for this. Why couldn't she have gone to some tropical island and set up a medical clinic? Oh no, she had to throw herself into one of the world's hottest trouble spots. It would be just like her to get herself killed.

Ian hadn't fooled him, either. Molly's father was worried sick about her himself, and Jordan had fallen right into the old man's capable hands, coming to see him when he did. Talk about crummy timing. He should get some kind of award for that.

"Molly's in Manukua," Jordan announced to Lesley without warning.

"Manukua," Lesley repeated in an astonished gasp. "What in the name of heaven is she doing there?"

"She volunteered with some missionary group."

"Doesn't she realize how dangerous it is?" Lesley set her fork aside and reached for her wineglass. Jordan wished now that he'd taken more care breaking the news to her.

"I'm going after her." He didn't mention that Ian was pulling every string he had to get Jordan a visa. By hook or crook he was going to Manukua, even if he had to be smuggled into the country.

"You." Lesley's eyes went wide, and when she set the glass down the wine sloshed over the edge. "Jordan, that's ridiculous. Why should you be the one? If she's in any danger, then the State Department should be notified."

"Ian's aged considerably in the past three years and his health is too fragile for such a strenuous journey. Someone's got to do something, and soon, before Molly manages to get herself killed."

"But surely there's someone else who could go."

"No one Molly would listen to."

"But...what about your work?" It was rare to see Lesley so flustered.

"Paul Phelps will take over for me. I shouldn't be gone long—a week at the most."

"What about the necessary papers? My heavens, no one travels in and out of Manukua these days...do they? I mean, from what the newspeople are saying, the country's about to explode."

"Ian's making the arrangements for me. He'd intended on making the trip himself, against his doctor's and everyone else's advice. Listen, Lesley, this isn't anything I want to do. Trust me, if I was going to take a week away from the job, Manukua would be the last place I'd choose to visit."

"I understand, Jordan," she said, her hand reaching for his. "This is something you have to do."

Jordan's relief was so great his shoulders sagged with it. He hadn't been able to put his feelings into words, but Lesley had said it for him. Perfectly. It was something he needed to do. This one last thing before he said goodbye to this woman and their marriage. He considered going after Molly a moral obligation. To her and to Ian. To the man who'd given him advice and financial backing when he'd started out in construction. To the man who'd given him his daughter. Giving Molly back to Ian seemed a small thing to do by comparison.

"When do you leave?" Lesley asked, and Jordan noticed that her voice was shaking slightly, although she struggled to disguise it. Jordan was grateful she didn't attempt to talk him out of it, or to convince him of the danger he was placing himself in for a woman he intended to divorce.

"The first part of the week."

"So soon?"

"The sooner the better, don't you think?"

Lesley nodded, and lowered her eyes. "Just promise me one thing."

"Of course."

"Please be careful, because despite everything, I love you, Jordan Larabee."

Molly woke to the sound of gunfire echoing in the distance. She sat up in bed, but it took her a moment to orientate herself. Tossing aside the thin blanket, she climbed out of bed and quickly dressed. The rat-a-tat sounds seemed closer now and a shot of adrenaline propelled her into action.

Dawn had just come over the hill and Molly could see people running in several different directions at once. Pandemonium reigned.

"What's happening?" Molly demanded, catching an orderly by the shoulders.

Large brown eyes stared into hers. "The rebels are coming. You must go...now," he said urgently. "Very fast, do not wait."

"Dr. Morton?" Molly pleaded. "Have you seen Dr. Morton?"

He shook his head wildly, then broke away, running toward the row of parked vehicles.

"Richard," Molly shouted. She couldn't, wouldn't, leave without her friend. His sleeping quarters were across the compound from her own, but making her way across the open area was nearly impossible. Sounds came at her from every direction. People were shouting in more languages than she could understand. Fear was like an animal that clawed at her legs, nearly immobilizing her.

"Molly, Molly." Her name seemed to come from a deep valley. She whirled around to find Richard Morton frantically searching the crowd for her.

"Here," she shouted, waving her hand high above her head.

She had to fight her way to his side. Briefly, they clung to each other.

"We have to leave right away. Mwanda has a truck waiting."

Molly nodded, her hand gripping Richard's. They'd been fools not to heed headquarters' warnings. She'd worked with these people for two years and found them to be gentle, peace-loving souls. The dangers of a coup had seemed like distant threats that didn't affect her, but she was wrong.

"What about the sick?" Molly pleaded. Richard was on one side of her and the six-foot Mwanda on the other.

"We will care for them," Mwanda promised in halting English. "But first you go."

Richard and Molly were literally tossed into the truck bed. They huddled in the corners and waited for their escape, although only God knew what they'd meet along the way.

The truck fired to life. Molly swore the old camouflage contraption had served in Africa during World

War II. She was convinced God and Mwanda were the only ones who kept it running.

A tall, thin Manukuan boy vaulted toward the truck, speaking furiously in his native tongue. Over the past couple of years, Molly had picked up a fair amount of the language, although she wasn't as fluent as she would have liked. The cold hand of fear settled over her as her mind translated the frantic words.

Her gaze met Dr. Morton's and it was plain he understood the message, as well.

They couldn't leave now. It was too late. The countryside was swarming with rebel troops, bent on hatred and vengeance. Many innocents had already been murdered.

Richard and Molly were trapped inside the compound.

Mwanda turned off the engine and climbed out of the truck. His eyes were empty as he helped the two climb down from the back.

"What will we do now?" Molly asked.

Richard shrugged. "Wait."

Wait for what? was the immediate question that came to Molly's mind. For death, and pray that it would be merciful? She doubted that there was any real chance of rescue now. If they were captured, what they might do to her as a woman didn't bear thinking.

So this was how it was to be for her. Surprisingly she wasn't afraid. The fear left her as quickly as it came, replaced with an incredible sense of calm. If the rebels broke through the compound, they weren't going to find her cowering in some corner. They'd find her doing what she did each and every day, helping her patients.

"I believe I'll do my rounds," Richard announced, his voice shaking slightly.

"I'll come with you," Molly said.

Her partner seemed pleased to have the company and offered her a shaky smile.

Mwanda shook his head and, with a resigned shrug of his shoulders, moved away. "I go back to kitchen," he announced with a wide smile. Two of his teeth were missing, but Molly doubted that she'd ever seen him smile more brightly. Or bravely.

Clinging to routine was of primary importance to them; although the thread of normalcy was fragile and threatened to break at any moment, it was all they had to hold on to.

The sound of gunfire continued to sound in the distance, creeping closer, bit by bit. Radio communication with Makua had been severed, so they had no way of knowing what was happening in the capital city. For all Molly knew, the entire country had been taken over.

It was the not knowing that was the worst. Several of their patients left, preferring to take their chances on reaching their families. Richard tended to those who were too sick to walk away from the compound. Several attempted to convince Molly and Richard to leave with them, but they refused. This was where they belonged. This was where they'd stay. Within minutes, Molly was shocked to realize there was only a handful of natives left.

Molly prayed for their safety, but there was no way for them to know how long they'd be safe behind the protective walls of the compound.

It could have been minutes, but it might have been hours later, when Molly heard the unmistakable sounds of a helicopter. It circled the compound, but she couldn't read any markings on it, so she wasn't sure if it was friend or foe.

The chopper hovered, then slowly descended. The noise was deafening, and the wind strong enough to stir up a thick layer of red dirt that cut visibility down to practically zero.

From the snatches of color she did manage to glimpse, she saw soldiers leap from the helicopter, dressed in full battle gear. Guerrillas, she suspected.

Molly remained in the pediatric ward, empty now. The door burst open and she faced a soldier with a machine gun. The guerilla stopped when he saw her, then shouted something over his shoulder. Molly straightened her shoulders and waited, not knowing for what.

A few seconds later another man burst into the room, nearly tearing the door off its hinges in his rush. Bracing herself against the rails of a crib, she met the angry eyes and realized they were hazel. And amazingly familiar.

"Jordan?" she whispered, looking up into the tight features of her husband. "What are you doing here?"

Chapter Two

"We're getting the hell out of here," Jordan said, convinced his heart rate was in excess of ninety miles an hour. From the aerial view he'd gotten from the helicopter, the rebels looked to be less than two or three miles outside of the medical compound and were quickly gaining territory. It was likely they'd move in on them at any minute.

"What about Richard?" Molly cried. "I can't leave without him."

"Who?" Jordan argued, gripping her by the upper arm and half lifting, half dragging her toward the door. Zane, and the men his mercenary friend had hired, surrounded the helicopter, their machine guns poised and ready.

"Dr. Morton," Molly shouted to be heard above the roar of the whirling blades of the helicopter. "I can't leave without Richard."

"We don't have time," Jordan argued.

With surprising strength, Molly tore herself away; her eyes were bright with fire as she glared at him. "I refuse to go without him."

"This is a hell of a time to be worrying about your boyfriend, don't you think?" Jordan snapped, furious that she'd be concerned about another man when he was risking his damn fool neck to save hers.

"I'll get him," Molly said, surging past him. Before Jordan could stop her she was gone. The helicopter blades stirred up a thick fog of dust and smoke. Bedlam surrounded them. An ominous crackling noise could be heard in the distance. More than once Jordan had asked himself what craziness had possessed his wife to put herself into this situation. Molly wasn't the only one—he was stuck in Manukua, as well, and wishing the hell he was just about anyplace else.

Jordan's area of expertise lay in constructing highrise apartments and office buildings. Guerrilla warfare was definitely out of his league and the very reason he'd contacted Zane Halquist.

"Molly," he shouted, shaking with urgency, "there isn't time."

Either she didn't hear him, or she chose to ignore his frantic call. It came to him that he should leave without her. He would have, too, if he'd known he could live with himself afterward. This woman was going to be the end of him yet. Jordan had never thought of himself as a coward, but he sure as hell felt like one now.

An explosion rang in his ears, the blast strong enough to knock him off-balance and jar his senses. He staggered a few steps before he caught himself. He shook his head, hoping that would help bring order to his thoughts. It didn't.

Zane shouted something to him, but with his ears ringing, Jordan didn't have a prayer of understanding him. He shook his head to indicate as much, but by that time it wasn't necessary. The man he'd trusted, the man he'd freely handed several thousand American dollars, raced toward the waiting copter with two or three of the other soldiers.

Jordan's heart slammed against his chest when he realized what was happening. They were leaving him, Molly and a handful of mercenaries behind.

Jordan hadn't finished cursing when he saw Molly with an elderly man on the far side of the compound. She held her hand to her face to protect her eyes from the swirling dust. She stood frozen with shock and regret, he guessed, as she watched the helicopter lift and speed away.

The man who'd found Molly in the nursery grabbed Jordan by the elbow, jerking him out of his momentary paralysis. "Take the woman and hide," he instructed roughly.

Jordan's instinct was to stay and fight. He wasn't the type to sit contentedly on the sidelines and do nothing. "I'll help," Jordan insisted.

"Hide the woman first."

Jordan nodded and ran as if a machine gun were firing at his heels. He raced toward Molly, and she ran toward him. He caught her just as she stumbled and fell into his arms.

She clung to him and Jordan wove his fingers into her hair, pressing her against him. His heart pounded with fear and adrenaline.

Jordan had never been more angry with anyone in his life, and at the same identical moment he was so grateful she was alive he felt like breaking into tears. It amazed him that it had been more than three years since he'd last held her and that she fit like a comfortable glove in his embrace.

"Where can I hide you?"

She looked up at him blankly, then shook her head. "I...I don't know. The supply house, but wouldn't that be the first place anyone would look?"

Jordan agreed with her. "There isn't a cellar or something?"

"No."

"Then don't worry about it. If the rebels make it into the compound, they'll check every outbuilding. I'll take you and Dr. Morton to the supply hut."

"What about you?" She clenched his arm with a strength he found amazing, as if he were her lifeline.

"I'll be back later."

Her hands framed his face, and she blinked through a wall of tears. "Be careful please, be careful."

He nodded. He had no intention of sacrificing his life. Hand in hand they ran for the supply house. Jordan glanced around for Dr. Morton and saw that the men had taken Molly's friend under their wing and were hiding the elderly physician themselves.

The supply hut was locked, but luckily Molly had the key. Jordan quickly surveyed the grounds, wondering exactly how much protection this ramshackle building would offer her. If the rebels broke into the compound, he needed to be in a position where he could protect her.

The sound of gunfire rang in the distance, sounding like the cap guns he'd played with as a boy. Only this was real.

"Keep your head down," Jordan instructed, closing the door after her. "I'll be back for you as soon as I can." He noticed how pale and frightened she was, but that couldn't be helped. He probably didn't look much better himself. His last thought as he left her was that anyone going after Molly would need to kill him first.

Terror gripped Molly at every burst of a machine gun. She was huddled in the corner, hunched down, with her back against the wall, her knees tucked under her chin. Her hands covered her ears, and she gnawed on her lower lip until she tasted blood. The room was pitch-dark with only a thin ribbon of light that crept in from beneath the door.

Footsteps pounded past the storehouse and she stopped breathing for fear the rebels had succeeded and broken into the compound. The worst part of this ordeal was being alone. She wouldn't be nearly as frightened if Dr. Morton was with her. Or Jordan.

Nothing in this world could have shocked her more than her husband bursting into the nursery, armed with a rifle and dressed as if he were part of Special Forces. He'd served in the military, but that had been years earlier, when he was right out of high school.

She didn't know what craziness had possessed Jordan to risk his life to save her. It might sound ungrateful, but she'd rather he'd stayed in Chicago. He was furious with her, that much she'd read in his eyes, but then his anger wasn't anything new. In the end, before she'd moved out, their marriage had deteriorated to the point that they were barely on speaking terms. It hadn't always been like that. Only after Jeff had died . . . She forcefully pushed thoughts of their child from her mind. Early on in their marriage they'd been so deeply in love that Molly would never have believed anything would ever come between them.

Death had.

The grim reaper's scythe had struck and his blade had fallen directly between them, separating them in the most painful of ways, by claiming their six-month-old child.

Molly had no idea how much time had passed before the door opened. Panic gripped her as she squinted into the light, but she relaxed when she realized it was Jordan.

"What's happening?" she pleaded, eager for news.

"The hell if I know." He abruptly pulled the door closed after him. The room went dark once more and he lit a match that softly illuminated the compact quarters. He leaned his rifle against the wall and sank down onto the dirt floor next to her. She noted that his breathing was heavy. His shoulders heaved several times before he exhaled sharply and relaxed. "Knowing Zane, he'll do everything he can to come back for us, but there are no guarantees."

"Who the hell is Zane?"

"An old friend," he said, "you don't know him. We met in the Army years ago."

The room was pitch-black once more. His shoulders pressed against hers, and some of the terror and loneliness left her at his closeness. "What about the rebels?" She needed to know where they stood, or if there was any chance of them getting out of this alive. Death didn't concern her, but how she died did.

"Apparently Zane and the others have been able to hold them off, for now at least, but there're a thousand unknowns in this. Everything's quiet for the moment, but I don't expect that to last."

She nodded, although there wasn't any way he had of seeing her. "What are you doing here in Manukua?" The question had burned in her mind from the moment he'd stormed into the compound as if he were Rambo on the loose.

"Someone had to do something to get you out of here. Ian's worried sick. If you want to risk your own foolish neck, fine, but you might have waited until your father was too senile to know or care. He'd never recover if anything happened to you."

The words were thrown at her, an accusation, sharp and cutting in their intensity.

"I certainly didn't know anything like this was going to happen," she snapped back defensively.

"You might have opted to volunteer for someplace other than Manukua," he said between clenched teeth. "Why couldn't you be content dispensing medication to school kids? Oh no, that would have been too simple. What'd you do, look for the hottest trouble spot on the world map and aim for there?"

He was stiff and distant. It pained her to realize that, within five minutes of seeing each other after three years apart, they were arguing.

Molly knew that at some point in the future she'd need to talk with Jordan, she just hadn't suspected it would be here in Manukua, surrounded by rebel troops.

"I'm sorry you're involved in this," she said softly, and despite her best efforts her voice was swamped with emotion. Her words came out sounding as if she were standing at the bottom of a deep pit.

"It isn't your fault I'm here. I volunteered to come." The anger was gone out of his voice, as well, and she sensed his regret for his earlier outburst.

"H-how have you been?" she asked softly. It seemed insane that they would sit on the hard dirt floor of a run-down shack and exchange niceties. Especially when they were in danger of being attacked by rebel soldiers any minute. But Molly sincerely wanted to know how his life had been going these past few years.

"Busy."

"Are you still working twelve-hour days?"

"Yeah."

Molly figured as much. Jordan had never allowed himself to grieve openly for Jeff. He'd buried himself in his work, effectively closing himself off from her and from life. Not that she'd been any saint. After Jeff had died, she'd been consumed with guilt and was so emotionally needy a thousand Jordans couldn't have filled the void her son's death had left in her life.

As the weeks and months wore on after the funeral, Molly had become continually more lethargic, while Jordan took the business world by storm. Within eight months he was Chicago's golden boy, with his hand in three major construction projects. Meanwhile, Molly had trouble finding the energy to climb out of bed in the morning.

A gunshot echoed like cannon fire and Molly jerked instinctively.

"Relax," Jordan advised. "Everything's under control."

He couldn't know that, but she appreciated the reassurance. "I feel like such a fool," she admitted, pressing her forehead to her knee.

Jordan placed his arm around her shoulders and brought her closer to his side. His shoulder was rock hard, but his comfort was more welcome than a goosedown pillow. It was hard to imagine how two people who had desperately loved each other had grown so far apart. In all her life, however long or short it was to be, Molly didn't ever expect to love anyone as much as she had her husband and her son. It seemed vitally important Jordan know this. She couldn't leave matters as they were between them. Not when she'd been given the opportunity to make things right. The words felt like a huge lump in her throat. "If... if the worst does happen, I want you to know I'll always love you, Jordan."

He went still and quiet, as if he wasn't sure how to deal with her confession. "I've tried not to love you," he admitted grudgingly. "Somehow I never quite succeeded."

Another gunshot sounded, and in a knee-jerk reaction she burrowed deeper into the shelter of his arms. She trembled and Jordan increased the pressure, holding her tightly against him.

Burying her face in the hollow of his neck, she breathed in the warm, manly scent of him. Jordan said nothing, but continued to hold her as his arm gently caressed her back.

It had been so long since she'd been in her husband's arms, so long since she'd felt loved and protected. She might never have the opportunity again. This time together was like a gift God had given them both. Tears welled in her eyes and spilled down her cheek.

"Molly, don't cry. It'll be all right, I promise you."

"I'm not worried," she lied, "you're here and you always did love playing the role of the hero."

He brushed the hair away from her temple, his touch gentle and reassuring. She wanted to thank him for being here with her, but couldn't find the words to adequately express her gratitude.

Kissing his neck seemed the natural thing to do. She slid the tip of her tongue over his flesh, reveling in the salty taste of him. She felt him tense, but he didn't stop her, nor did he encourage her.

Her palm was pressed against his heart and his pulse beat in strong, even thuds, the tempo increasing when she opened her mouth against the strong cord of his neck and sucked gently.

"Molly," he warned hoarsely, his hands gripping her upper arms as if to push her away. He'd done that often enough after Jeff's death, as if his desire for her had died with his son. Perhaps not physically, but emotionally.

"I'm sorry..." she whispered, but before she could say anything more, his mouth was on hers, hot and compelling. His kiss was so fierce that her breath jammed in her throat and her nails dug into his shoulders.

Molly knew that it was crazy for them to get involved in something like this now, but it didn't stop her from responding, didn't keep her from moaning in abject surrender. She returned his kisses with a wildness that had been carefully hidden and denied for three long years.

Jordan stroked her breasts, his touch feather light, as if he were afraid of what would happen if he allowed himself to enjoy the fruits of her body. Her nipples quivered until they hardened and throbbed for his touch. Molly needed him as she had rarely needed anyone. Her fingers awkwardly reached for the buttons of her blouse, unfastening them in haste and peeling it off her shoulders. Jordan helped her remove her bra and groaned hoarsely as her breasts spilled into his waiting palms.

"Molly..."

"Love me," she pleaded softly. "One last time ... I need you so much."

His mouth fastened on her nipple with greedy passion. Wild sensation shot through her and she buckled at the mixture of pleasure and pain. He feasted on one nipple and then the other, suckling and bunching her breasts together while his mouth created a slick, well-traveled trail between the two hardened peaks.

"This is nuts." Jordan sighed, but he didn't reveal any signs of putting an end to it.

"The world is crazy," she reminded him and finished undressing.

His hand moved lower, caressing her smooth abdomen and flat stomach, edging downward until he reached the soft patch of hairs between her thighs. He flattened his hand there as if to absorb the pulsations that rocked her. It was as though the years apart had vanished like mist. They were well acquainted with each other's bodies and used that knowledge to drive one another to a fever pitch of desire and need.

Seated, he positioned her on top of him. The sounds outside the supply shed were lost to the thunder of her heart echoing in her ears and the soft moaning sounds working their way up the back of her throat.

They were on fire for each other as he slowly lowered her onto the swollen strength of his manhood. His hands dug into her hips as she swallowed him with her own moist heat.

Molly gasped with pleasure, thinking she would die with it. Her head fell forward, her hair spilling wildly over her face.

It had been so long, so very long, since they'd last made love. A sob of welcome and regret was trapped in her chest as Jordan worked her against him, setting the cadence for their lovemaking.

A few moments later Jordan growled, then panted as if struggling for control. His breath came in short, uneven gasps as she rotated her hips against him, tormenting him the same way he was her. His hands closed over her buttocks, controlling her thrusts, setting the rhythm, increasing the pace.

Danger surrounded them, the threat of death was very real, but there wasn't room in her mind for anything more than the wonder of their love, and the need they were satisfying with each other.

She cried out as her body reached its climax and Jordan clamped his mouth over hers, swallowing her cries of exultation and joy. Pleasure burst gloriously inside her even as the tears rained unheeded down her face.

Jordan responded with one savage thrust as he reached his own peak. Trembling, they clung to each other. Molly was sobbing softly against his shoulder and his arms were wrapped securely around her.

They didn't speak. There was no need; words would have been superfluous just then. Gently he kissed her, once and then again, not with passion but with thanksgiving. Molly returned his kisses with the same heartfelt gratitude.

Jordan helped her dress and held her close for several moments afterward. When he released her, she felt his reluctance. "I have to go," he told her.

"Where?" she cried, not wanting him to leave her.

"I'll be back as soon as I can," he promised, kissing her. "Trust me, Molly, I don't want to leave you, but I've already stayed longer than I should have."

"I understand." She tried to hide, without much success, the panic she felt.

He brushed his hand against her temple, running his fingers down the side of her face. "I won't be long, I promise."

She knew he didn't want to leave any more than she wanted to see him go, but it was necessary. For the safety of them both.

Once she was alone, Molly shut her eyes and prayed God would protect her husband. She'd lost track of time and didn't know if it was afternoon or evening. The light coming from beneath the door seemed less bright, but that could be her imagination.

Jordan returned several hours later with blankets and food. Although she hadn't eaten all day, Molly wasn't hungry. Only because he insisted did she manage to down the MREs, meals ready to eat, he brought with him. Leave it to a man to think of food at a time like this. Jordan ate ravenously, while she picked at her food.

"What's happening around the compound?" she asked, finishing off a piece of dried fruit.

"It's secure for now."

"What about Dr. Morton?"

"He's safe and asking about you." He spread the blanket over the dirt floor. "Try and get some sleep," he advised. "Here." He wrapped his arm around her shoulders and brought her close to his side, but something was different. His hold wasn't as tight nor as personal as it had been earlier.

"Jordan," she asked, nestling close. "Are you sorry about what happened before? Neither of us planned on making love and, well, I thought it might be troubling you."

"No, I don't regret it." His answer sounded oddly defensive. "But I should."

"Why? Good grief, we're married."

He didn't answer her right away. "It's been three years. A lot can happen in that amount of time."

"I know."

"I'm not the same person anymore."

"Neither am I," she agreed.

After the hellish fighting of the day, the night seemed relatively peaceful. The sounds of silence were welcome ones. For the first time since Jordan had made love to her earlier, she felt safe and protected. Whatever happened didn't matter as long as she was in his arms.

Molly's breasts inadvertently brushed against the hard wall of his chest and Jordan's breath caught. It seemed several moments passed before he breathed again.

He kissed her once, softly, experimentally, then again and again, each kiss gaining in length and intensity. He slid his mouth from her lips across her cheek to her ear, taking the lobe between his teeth and sucking gently. Molly gasped as the tingly sensation rippled down her spine.

Jordan chuckled softly. "I wondered if that had changed."

"Two can play that game, buster." She climbed into his lap and placed her head against his shoulder. Wrapping her arms around his neck, she spread a series of soft kisses along the underside of his jaw, using her tongue to tease and entice him. She didn't need any lights to know the effect she was having on him. Jordan couldn't disguise his growing need.

He kissed her then as if he were starving for her. His tongue alternately plundered and caressed her mouth while he locked his arms around her waist and her back. It was as if Jordan never intended on letting go of her again. It was a feeling Molly could learn to live with.

She met his hunger with her own and soon their passion became a raging fire that threatened to consume them both. Their bodies had found satisfaction in each other only hours earlier and yet it wasn't adequate to quench the long dry spell away from each other.

They couldn't take off their clothes fast enough, removing only what was necessary. Jordan spoke, but Molly found the words strangled and incomprehensible. Not that it mattered; nothing did just then, except each other.

Their desire for one another was urgent and frantic, and Jordan's strength might have bruised her if she had been aware of anything beyond her own tortuous need. As had happened earlier, Molly found her deliverance first and buried her face in the warm hollow of his neck. Soon afterward Jordan's body shuddered and she felt his throbbing release deep inside her body. She moved against him, her thighs clenched as she milked him in a driving dance of ecstasy. The melting sensation increased her own lingering enjoyment.

Molly didn't know how much time elapsed before her breathing returned to normal.

"I can't believe this," Jordan murmured between soft, gentle kisses.

"Who would have thought we'd experience the most incredible sex of our lives in a supply hut in Africa?" she whispered. If the soldiers burst in and gunned her down right then and there, Molly decided she'd die a happy woman. She doubted that either of them could have mustered the strength to put up much of a fight.

"You're smiling?" Jordan asked, pushing the hair away from her face.

"You would be, too, if you experienced anything close to what I just did."

"Trust me, I'm smiling."

"You know what I was thinking," she said, then yawned loudly.

"What?"

"I just realized I'd really like to come out of this mess alive."

"So would I," Jordan said adamantly.

That hadn't been entirely true for Molly. She didn't actively think about death, but she hadn't much cared what happened, either. One way or the other it hadn't seemed to matter. It did now, and she had Jordan to thank for that.

"Do you think you can sleep now?" he asked, his hands stroking her back.

She nodded. "What about you?"

"Yeah, for a while. I've got the second watch. My feeling is we'll know more about what's going to happen in the morning."

Nestled against him, warm and snug, Molly felt herself drifting off. Sleep would have been impossible earlier, now it came to her like an unexpected gift.

Sometime later, she felt Jordan leave. He kissed her softly before slipping out of the storehouse. She didn't remember anything else until he returned. He climbed beneath the single blanket and lay down beside her, gathering her close. His arm slipped over her middle and cupped her breast. Molly felt his sigh as he relaxed and she smiled softly to herself. It was almost as if the past three years hadn't happened. It was almost as if they were young and in love all over again. Almost as if Jeff hadn't died.

Molly woke to the unmistakable sound of gunfire. It was close. Much closer than before, as if a war had erupted outside the door.

Jordan bolted upright and reached for his weapon. "Stay here," he ordered and was gone before she could protest.

Molly barely had time to gather her wits when the door to the shed was thrust open. Jordan stood framed in the light. "Come on," he shouted, holding out his hand to her. "Zane's coming and this time we're going with the chopper."

Molly was so relieved that she would have gladly kissed Jordan's friend. He was coming back! She could hear the chopper more distinctly when she moved outside of the supply shed. She was greeted with a whirlwind of dust and grit. Doing what she could to protect her eyes, she hunched forward and, with Jordan's arm around her waist guiding her, ran for all she was worth toward the deafening sound.

Dr. Morton climbed into the helicopter after her, looking shaken and exhausted. He offered her a weak smile and gently patted her hand as he moved to the rear of the aircraft. Molly waited for Jordan, but he didn't board with the other soldiers.

"Where's my husband?" she demanded.

"He's coming. Don't worry, Jordan can take care of himself." He guided her firmly but gently out of harm's way.

"Jordan," Molly shouted, near frantic. The chopper was filling up with people and she couldn't find her husband. Pushing her way past the others, Molly was sobbing when she saw him. He was walking backward toward the chopper, his gun raised and firing at what she could only guess.

The chopper started to lift.

"Jordan," she screamed, although there wasn't a prayer he could hear her. "For the love of God, hurry."

Some part of her must have reached him because he turned abruptly and ran like she'd never seen him sprint before, racing toward the chopper. The minute his back was turned three rebels appeared from around the end of the hospital. Two men fired machine guns from the door of the chopper while Zane helped lift and drag Jordan aboard. He collapsed once inside, pale and bleeding heavily from his shoulder. He hand clenched his wound and the blood oozed between his fingers.

Molly fell at his side, weeping. "You've been hit."

He smiled weakly up at her, then his eyelids fluttered closed. He'd passed out cold.

Chapter Three

Jordan felt as if his shoulder were on fire. The pain seared a path through his mind, catching hold of him and guiding him out of the comfort of the black void.

He opened his eyes to find Molly and her physician friend working over him. Bright red blotches of blood coated the front of her blouse and he guessed it was his own. She seemed to sense that he was awake and paused to look toward his face.

"You're going to be fine," she assured him when she realized he'd regained consciousness. But Jordan wasn't so out of it that he didn't recognize the cold fear in her eyes.

"Liar," he said, and the lone word demanded every ounce of strength he possessed. Even then his voice was little more than a husky whisper.

Molly held his hand between her own, her eyes bright with tears. "Rest if you can. Zane said we'll be to Nubambay soon. There's an excellent hospital there."

"Nubambay," he repeated weakly.

"Don't worry, the country's government is safe and sound."

He attempted a smile.

"I won't let anything more happen to you, Jordan, do you understand? It's over now."

He closed his eyes, tried to nod, but it required more energy than he could muster. The pain in his shoulder increased and he gritted his teeth with the agony. Then gratefully everything started to go black. Jordan welcomed the release, sighing as the bottomless void settled over him.

When he awoke again, the first things Jordan saw were an IV bottle and stark white walls. The antiseptic scent assured him he was in a hospital.

He blinked and rolled his head to one side. Molly was asleep in the chair next to his hospital bed. How she could rest in a molded plastic chair was beyond him. She'd curled up in a tight ball, her feet tucked beneath her. Her head rested against her shoulder and a thick strand of beautiful golden hair fell across her cheek. With her pale blond hair and bright blue eyes, she must have caused a stir with the children of Manukua, he mused, especially if they'd never seen a white woman before.

Molly was a natural with children, Jordan remembered. Once she found it in her heart to forgive herself for what happened to Jeff, there was a chance she'd marry again and have the family she'd always wanted.

A weight settled over his chest, as heavy as a concrete barricade. He'd done his stint with this fatherhood business and wasn't willing to take the risk a second time.

Lesley had agreed there would be no children. He was convinced they'd find their happiness together.

Molly was a different kind of woman. She was a natural mother, and in time she would be again. Jordan remembered when they'd first brought Jeff home from the hospital. He'd been afraid to hold their son for fear he'd inadvertently do something to hurt him.

By contrast Molly had acted as if she'd been around infants all her life. She'd laughed off his concerns and taught him what he needed to know, insisting he spend part of each day holding and talking to Jeff. Soon he was as comfortable as she was and the nightly sessions he spent with Jeff had been the highlight of his day. Jeff had been a happy baby with a budding personality.

Then he was gone.

Unexpectedly he'd been ripped from their lives without rhyme or reason, leaving behind a burden of grief and anger that had crippled them both. What an unfortunate legacy for such a cheerful, good-natured baby.

Jordan forced himself to look away from Molly. He closed his eyes and with some difficulty brought Lesley's face to his mind. Sweet, kind Lesley. A fuzzy image drifted carelessly into his conscious, followed by a deepening sense of guilt.

He'd made love to Molly, not once but twice. A momentary lapse in good judgment he could explain away, but not two such breaches. Not that he was obliged to explain anything to Lesley. She wasn't the type to ask, and he sure as hell wasn't going to volunteer any confessions.

"Jordan?" His name came to him softly, tentatively, as if Molly were afraid to wake him.

He rolled his head toward her. "Hi," he said, and realized his mouth felt as if someone had stuffed it full of cotton balls.

"How are you feeling?" She stood by his side and gently stroked his forehead.

"Like hell."

"Are you thirsty?"

He nodded. It surprised him how well she anticipated his needs.

"Here." She poured him a glass of ice water and brought it to him with a straw. She held it to his mouth and he drank greedily, letting the cold water quench the bulk of his thirst.

"All right," he said, relaxing against the pillows once he'd drank his fill. "Let's talk about the bullet. How much damage did it do?"

"There were two and both of them were clean hits. Luckily there's no bone damage. It's going to hurt like hell for a while, but you'll recover. Think of this time as a long overdue vacation."

"This may come as something of a surprise," Jordan said, having trouble hiding his agitation, "but if I'm going to vacation I'd prefer a nice peaceful Caribbean island instead of fighting off rebels bent on mayhem."

"I couldn't agree with you more. I could arrange for us to fly to the Virgin Islands. A couple of weeks there soaking up the sun and the sand would do us both good." Her eyes brightened with the idea. He could almost see the little wheels churning in her mind, stirring up some romantic fantasy she was dying to live out.

Jordan closed his eyes. He'd walked into that one all by himself and had sank to his thighs in the thick mud of the past. There wasn't anyway in hell he could spend two weeks in paradise with Molly when he fully intended on going through with the divorce.

"How soon can I travel?" he asked roughly.

"A couple of days. You're weak now because of the blood loss, but with the proper rest you'll regain your strength soon enough."

"I have to get back to Chicago. I don't have time to lollygag around some beach."

"All right."

Jordan heard the hurt and disappointment in her voice and felt like a jerk. That compounded with everything else left him feeling sick to his stomach. He never intended to make love to Molly; he never intended on getting shot up, either.

"How soon can I get the hell out of here?" he wanted to know next. The question came out sounding gruff and impatient. He felt both. The sooner he could make the break between him and Molly the better. Unfortunately he'd ruined any chance of making it a clean one.

"You should be released the day after tomorrow," Molly told him. "I've booked a hotel room and will call and arrange the flight back to the States if you want."

"I want." Jordan couldn't put it any more bluntly than that.

Molly walked over to the window and gazed out. She crossed her arms and waited a couple of moments before asking, "Why are you so angry?"

"Maybe it's because I've got two bullet holes in my shoulder. Then again it might be because I was forced to fly halfway around the world to get you when you should have had the common sense to leave on your own. It's you who's got the death wish, not me.''

"I didn't ask you to come," she flared.

"No, your father did."

"Next time I suggest you stay at home," she said heatedly as she walked past the bed. She moved so speedily that he felt a draft.

"Next time I will," he called after her, his voice little more than a thin reed of sound.

Jordan didn't see her again until it was time for him to be released from the hospital. Zane stopped in later, but Jordan wasn't in the mood for company. The two shook hands and Jordan didn't expect to see his friend again.

Molly was at the hospital a number of times. He heard her talking to the doctor outside his room once and she stopped in to sit with him when he was sleeping. He wasn't sure how he knew this, he just did.

Jordan wasn't a good patient in the best of times. He was convinced that by the time he left Nubambay Hospital the staff was more than ready to be rid of him. Not that he blamed anyone. He'd been a rotten patient; he knew it and regretted it.

Molly was waiting for him outside the room with a wheelchair.

"I'll walk," he insisted.

"Jordan, for the love of heaven, be sensible."

He threw her a look that told her if he had any real sense he would have stayed in Chicago.

The cab ride to the hotel seemed to take hours. By the time they arrived he was exhausted, much too tired to complain that she'd booked them in one room. At least there were twin beds.

Molly ordered lunch from room service and they ate in silence. Jordan didn't plan on it, but he fell asleep afterward and woke up two hours later.

Molly was gone, which was just as well. He was uncomfortable around her. If he wasn't such a coward he'd talk to her about the divorce and get it out in the open the way he'd originally intended. Somehow it didn't seem the right thing following their night in the supply shed. Their lovemaking episodes had definitely put a chink in that plan. He didn't know what the hell he was going to do now.

Sitting on the end of the bed, Jordan carefully worked one shoulder and then the other. Pain ripped through him and he gritted his teeth. The medication the doctor gave him was in the bathroom and he walked in there without thinking.

He realized his mistake the moment he stepped over the threshold. Molly was in the shower, standing under the spray of warm water and lathering her torso. The muted glass did little to hide her lush figure from him. Her creamy, smooth skin glowed and her breasts stood out proud and regal, her nipples a deep rose color beaded against the force of the water. She lathered the washcloth and rubbed it over her stomach and lower between her legs, parting her thighs.

Jordan's breath caught in his throat, and he reached out and gripped hold of the sink. He was instantly aroused. This had to be some sort of punishment God had seen fit to place upon him for his many sins.

The view of his wife hypnotized him, and for the life of him Jordan couldn't force himself to look away. He could barely control the need he felt to touch her and taste her again. It was impossible for reality to live up to the memory of her in his arms, her legs wrapped around his hips. He meant to turn and walk out as abruptly as he'd entered, but his legs were heavy and rooted him there.

"Jordan?"

"Sorry," he muttered, feeling like a schoolboy caught with his hand in the cookie jar, "I didn't mean to interrupt you."

"It's no problem." She turned off the water and reached out and grabbed a towel, taking it into the shower with her.

Jordan stood transfixed, unable to manage more than the simple breath, as she dried her arms and breasts. Something was very wrong. Jordan was a strong-willed man. He wasn't easily tempted by the flesh. The past three and a half years of celibacy were testament to that.

Somehow he managed to make it back into the other room. He literally fell into a chair and turned on the television. A full five minutes passed before he realized the broadcast was televised in French.

A couple of minutes later, Molly strolled barefoot out of the bathroom, dressed in a thick, white terrycloth robe. She toweled her hair dry and wore a silly grin as if she were fully aware of the affect she had on him. Apparently she enjoyed seeing him suffer.

"Did you need a pain pill?" she asked ever so sweetly.

Jordan shook his head and concentrated on the television screen as though he understood every word spoken.

Jordan had behaved strangely from the moment they'd left the medical compound in Manukua. Matters weren't any better now that they were on the flight headed back to Chicago.

Molly didn't know what to make of his irrational behavior. One moment he was looking at her as if he was counting the minutes before he could charm her into his bed and the next he growled at her.

Okay, she reasoned, so he had been wounded. He was an injured beast. Depending on his mood, she didn't know whether to comfort or clobber him. One minute he was sullen and uncommunicative, and the next witty and warm. Almost warm, she amended. Jordan had never been a personable kind of man. He was too direct and blunt for that.

He fidgeted in the cramped airline seat next to hers, trying to find a comfortable position. The pain pills would have helped him relax, if he'd agreed to take them. Molly had given up suggesting as much. The looks he sent her were enough to tell her exactly what he wanted her to do with the pain medication. He was a damn stubborn fool, and if he hadn't risked his life to save hers, she'd have told him so.

The newsmagazine Jordan was reading slid from his lap onto the floor. Molly retrieved it for him and he immediately crammed it into the pocket of the seat in front of him, bending it in half, then stuffing the excess pages down with a force strong enough to cause the seat to rock.

"Now, now," Molly said under her breath.

Jordan muttered something she preferred not to hear, then glanced at his watch, something he did routinely every five minutes or so. She thought to remind him of the old adage of a watched pot not boiling, but strongly suspected he wouldn't appreciate her pearls of wisdom.

An eternity passed before the plane touched down at O'Hare International. She was home and the joy that swelled in her chest was testament to how glad she was to be back.

Customs seemed to take forever. Her father was waiting for her, looking older than she remembered. His face lit up with a smile when she appeared and he held his arms open wide the way he had when she was a little girl.

"Daddy," she said, hugging him close. Unexpected tears welled in her eyes and, embarrassed, she wiped them aside. She clung to him, drinking in his love. She may be a mature woman, but she'd never outgrow her need for her father's love.

"It's about time you came back where you belong," Ian chastised, and wiped the moisture from his eyes. He hugged her again once more, then wrapped his arm around her waist.

Jordan shifted his weight from one foot to the other. He hated emotional scenes, Molly knew.

"Thank you," Ian said, breaking away from her and shaking Jordan's good hand. It took him a moment or two to compose himself before he was able to continue. "I might have lost my little girl if it hadn't been for you."

"It was no big deal," Jordan said as if he'd done nothing more than walk her across the street. A fuss would embarrass him, and so she discounted his heroism.

A porter walked past with Jordan's luggage and Jordan glanced outside, obviously eager to be on his way. His gaze met Molly's and in it she read a multitude of emotions. Relief that they were home and safe, regret, too, she suspected. His defenses were lower, dulled by pain and fatigue. He couldn't disguise his feelings from her as easily as he had in the past.

"Take care," Molly said, taking a step toward him before she could stop herself. She longed to press her hand to his cheek and thank him herself, as if it were possible to ever adequately express her appreciation. She longed to kiss him, too, to prove what they'd experienced had been as real as it had been right.

He nodded. "I will. I'll call you later in the week," he promised.

Molly had to bite her lip to keep from telling him not to work too hard. A gunshot wound wasn't a simple injury and it would be weeks, possibly months, before he regained the full use of his arm. She bit her lip; Jordan wouldn't have appreciated the admonition.

He turned abruptly then and followed the porter outside.

Molly watched him go. She'd lived apart from Jordan for three long years, considered their life together forever gone, destroyed by grief and pain. This week had shown her the impossible. This week proved beyond a shadow of question that Jordan continued to love her. Just as she did him.

He wasn't happy about it, she mused sadly. She sincerely doubted that he knew what he was going to do. For now he was as confused and uncertain as she was herself.

Molly woke with the sun rippling across the cherrywood dresser in the bedroom that had been hers as a young girl. She lay on her back, her head cradled by thick feather pillows, and reveled in the abundant comforts of home.

She wasn't a teenager any longer, but a woman. A married woman. The thought produced a small frown. Some decisions had to be made regarding her relationship with Jordan, but neither of them were ready to make those. Three years seemed plenty of time to decide what they were going to do with their relationship. In their case it wasn't.

Molly dressed in a sleeveless summer dress she found in the back of her closet. A pretty white-with-red-dots concoction with a wide belt.

Her father was sitting at the breakfast table with the morning newspaper propped up against his glass of freshly squeezed orange juice. It seemed little had changed in the years she'd been away.

"Morning," she said, kissing him on the cheek and pouring herself a cup of coffee.

"Morning" came his absent response.

"I see you still read over the financial section first thing every morning."

"I'm retired, not dead," he said with a chuckle. "Semiretired. I got too bored sitting at home, counting my money."

"So you're working again."

"Don't fuss," he said, his eyes not leaving the paper. "I go into the bank a couple of days a week. The staff there are kind enough to let me keep my office, so I go down and putter around and they let me think I'm important. I know otherwise, but I don't let on."

Molly smiled, pulled out a chair and sat down. Her father had always been big on formality. Lunch and dinner were served in the dining room on Wedgwood china and Waterford crystal. Breakfast, however, was taken in the kitchen at the round oak table that sat in a comfortable nook where the sunlight spilled in and splashed around them.

Molly reached for a blueberry muffin and the pitcher of orange juice. "Dad, did Jordan sell the house?"

Her father lowered the paper, folded it in fourths and set it beside his plate. "Not to my knowledge, why?"

She shrugged. "I was curious."

He studied her for a long moment. "I take it the two of you didn't get much chance to talk."

Peeling the paper bottom away from the muffin, Molly shook her head. "Not really." Her words were followed by a short silence.

"I see." Molly raised her gaze to her father. He sounded downright gleeful, as if this small bit of information were cause for celebration.

"What's the grin all about?" she asked.

"What grin?" His eyes went instantly sober, then round with innocence.

"Don't play games with me, Dad. Does Jordan have something to tell me?"

"I wouldn't know," he said and the edges of his mouth quivered ever so slightly. "Now," he added in a whisper.

Molly stood and set the napkin on the table, frowning. "Something fishy's going on here."

"Oh?"

She'd forgotten what a little devil her father could be. She walked over to the patio doors, crossed her arms and tapped her foot while she thought of the unexpected turn of the morning's events.

"Can I have the car keys?" she asked, whirling back around, her decision made.

Her father held them out in the palm of his hand, grinning broadly. "I won't expect you home for lunch,'' he said and reached once more for his morning paper.

It was ridiculous to show up on Jordan's doorstep before ten. Especially when he'd so recently arrived back from Africa. Unsure how to proceed, Molly drove to their favorite French bakery for croissants. To her surprise and delight, the baker, Pierre, recognized her. He called to her and hurried around the glass counter to shake her hand.

"I gave up hope of ever seeing you again," he said in a heavy French accent. He poured her a cup of coffee and led her to one of the small tables in the corner, in front of the long row of windows. "Please sit down."

Molly did, wondering at this unusual greeting. He set the coffee down and his assistant delivered a plate of delicate sweet rolls. The aroma was enticing enough to cause a weight gain.

"Our daughter's baby died the same way as your son," he said, and his eyes revealed the extent of his sadness. "Amanda put her little girl down to sleep and Christi never woke. It's been several months now and still my daughter and her husband grieve, still they ask questions no one can answer."

"The questions never stop," Molly said softly. Nor does the grief, but she didn't say that. It grew less sharp with time, the years dulled the agony, but it never left, never vanished. The pain was there, a constant reminder of the baby who never grew up.

"Our daughter and son-in-law blame themselves . . . they think they did something to cause Christi's death."

"They didn't." Molly was giving the textbook response, but in her heart she knew differently. The medical community had no cut-and-dried answers. Physicians offered a number of theories, but nothing concrete. There was no one to blame, no one to hold responsible, no one to yell and cry at, or take out their grief upon.

With nowhere else to go, the pain, anger and grief turned inward. It had with Molly, until she bore the full weight of the tragedy upon her thin shoulders. Over the months, the burden of it had maimed her. By the time she moved out on Jordan, she was an emotional wreck.

"They need to talk to someone who has lost a child the same way," Pierre said, "before this unfortunate death destroys them both." He stood and took a business card from the display in front of the cash register. Turning it over, he wrote a phone number on the back side.

Molly accepted the card, but she wasn't sure she could make the call. There were others this young couple could speak to, others far more qualified to answer their questions. Another husband and wife who'd walked over the fiery bed of coals and come out on the other side.

"Please," Pierre said, folding his much-larger hand around hers and the card. "Only someone who has lost a child can understand their pain."

"I . . . don't know, Pierre."

His eyes boldly met hers. "God will guide you," he said. "Do not worry." He brought her a sack with the croissants and wouldn't allow her to pay for them.

Molly left, not knowing what to do. If she hadn't been able to help herself or Jordan, how could she reach another grieving couple?

Jordan's truck was parked outside their home. So he hadn't sold the house. This small bit of information lifted her spirits. She didn't put much significance in his keeping the two-story house, but knowing this one piece of their marriage was intact was just the incentive she needed to propel her to the front steps.

This was the first time she'd been back and she wasn't sure if she should knock or simply walk inside. It was her home, or at least it had been at one time. Ringing the doorbell was the courteous thing to do.

It took Jordan an inordinate amount of time to answer. He opened the front door with a bathrobe draped over his naked shoulders. His hair stood on end and he blinked as if afraid she were an apparition.

"Before you chew my head off," she said, remembering what a grouch he was in the morning, "I come bearing gifts."

"This better be good," he said, eyeing the white sack.

"Pierre's croissants," she informed him.

He grinned, opening the screen door. "That's good enough."

The house was exactly as she'd left it. Sort of. The furniture was arranged in the identical pattern. Jordan hadn't updated the carpet or the drapes. Everything was as she'd left it except there were blueprints and files stacked in every conceivable corner.

"I see you still bring your work home with you," she commented dryly.

"Listen, if you came to lecture me, you can go right back out that door. Just leave the croissants—I deserve that much for answering the doorbell."

"Never mind," she said, leading the way into the kitchen. This room wasn't much better. Luckily she was familiar enough to know where he kept the coffee. She put on a pot, then brought down two black mugs embossed with silver—Larabee Construction.

"Hey," she teased, "you're in the big time now. When did you give up the pencils and go for the mugs?"

Jordan frowned at her and it was obvious he had no intention of answering her question. Molly found his surly mood entertaining. She waited until the coffee had filtered through, poured him a mug and carried it over to the table, where he'd planted himself.

He wolfed down two croissants before she managed to get hers out of the bag. The return of his appetite encouraged her. The temptation to ask him about his medication was strong, but she resisted, knowing he'd consider the query some sort of intrusion on his privacy.

"Dad asked me if we'd had a chance to talk," Molly said evenly, carefully broaching the subject.

Jordan stopped eating and his gaze narrowed.

"Was there some particular reason he seemed so curious about us talking?"

He took his own sweet time mulling over the question. Molly didn't press him, didn't force the issue. She knew Jordan well enough to realize that when and if he offered an explanation it would be in his time, not hers, and certainly not her father's.

The doorbell chimed once more. Jordan growled, stood and answered it. Paul Phelps, his job superintendent, casually strolled inside and paused when he saw Molly. His face lit up in a broad grin.

"Molly. Damn but it's good to see you." He walked over and gave her a bear hug. "You're a sight for sore eyes."

Molly had always enjoyed Paul, who was more friend than employee. "How's the family?" she asked.

"Brenda had another girl last year," Paul boasted proudly.

"Congratulations."

Jordan's employee turned to her husband. "I saw a truck parked outside and wondered if you'd gotten back," Paul said conversationally and helped himself to a cup of coffee. "What the hell happened to your arm?" he asked Jordan, gesturing toward the sling.

"Nothing a little time won't fix," Jordan muttered. "If a parade's going to march through here, I might as well get dressed." He didn't look happy about it, but Molly welcomed the time alone with Paul.

"How's he been?" she asked as soon as Jordan had vacated the room.

Paul shrugged. "Better the last year or so since he..." He stopped abruptly and glanced guiltily toward Molly. "Since, well, you know, since he hasn't been killing himself working every hour of the day and night."

"If this house is any indication, that's exactly what he has been doing."

"What happened to his shoulder?" Paul asked, and Molly wondered if it was a blatant effort to change the subject.

"He was shot," she said, "twice."

"Shot." Paul damn near dropped the coffee mug.

"It's a long story," Molly said.

"Longer than either of us has time to explain," Jordan said gruffly, appearing in the doorway. From the frustrated look in his eyes, Molly realized his dressing was more than he could handle alone. He needed help, but she doubted that he'd ask for it.

Paul glanced from one of them to the other, then set the coffee cup down on the counter. "I can see you two have lots to talk about. It was good to see you again, Molly. Damn good. Don't make yourself a stranger now, you hear?"

She nodded and walked him to the door. He seemed anxious to make a clean getaway, but she stopped him, her hand at his elbow. "What is it everyone's trying to hide from me?"

Paul looked decidedly uncomfortable. "That's something you'd better ask Jordan."

Molly fully intended on doing exactly that. Her husband's eyes met hers when she walked back into the kitchen. She read a certain look about him, one she didn't freely recognize. It seemed to be a mixture of determination and regret. One of anger and pride.

"Tell me," she said without emotion.

His eyes briefly left hers. "There was more than one reason I went to Manukua," he said evenly. "You're father asked me to bring you home."

"And?"

"And," he said, taking in a deep breath. "I came to ask for a divorce."

Chapter Four

Molly felt as if the floor had collapsed beneath her, sending her crashing into space.

Divorce.

Jordan had come to Manukua to ask her for a divorce.

Since Jeff's death Molly had learned a good many things about emotional pain. The numbness came first, deadening her senses from the rush of unbearable heartache that was sure to follow. Only later would she expect the full impact of Jordan's words to hit her. For now she welcomed the protection.

"I see," she managed, closing her eyes. She'd made such an unadulterated fool of herself, suggesting they vacation together on a tropical island as if they were lovers, as if their marriage had been given a second chance. Her face burned with humiliation, but she resisted the urge to bury her face in her hands. "You might have said something sooner, before I made such a fool of myself.''

"If anyone's a fool, it's me." Jordan's voice was filled with self-condemnation.

"No wonder you were in such a rush to get back to the States.'' It all made sense now, a painful kind of logical sense.

"I didn't mean to blurt it out like that.'' He walked to the far side of the room, his shoulders slumped with regret.

"I'm glad you did. Good heavens, who knows how long I would have continued making a complete ass of myself.'' Another thought occurred to her. "My father knows, doesn't he?'' An answer wasn't necessary. Paul did, as well. That explained the awkward way he'd answered her questions and his hasty exit.

"I know what you're thinking,'' Jordan muttered.

"I doubt that.'' How could he when she didn't know herself?

"You're wondering about what happened between us in the supply shed.'' His mouth tightened as if he dreaded bringing up the subject. "If you're looking for an apology I can't give you one. It happened. It shouldn't have, but it did, and I'm not sorry.''

"I'll admit it was a curious way of saying good-bye,'' she said with a small, short-lived laugh. She appreciated his honesty, knowing what it had cost him. "I ... I don't regret it, either.''

"I never meant to hurt you.''

"I know.'' Her feet felt as heavy as concrete fence posts. Walking to the front door required an incredible effort. She paused, her back to him when the realization hit her like a sledgehammer against the back of the head. "You've met another woman, haven't you?''

He didn't answer right away, in fact it seemed to take him a good long while to formulate a reply. Long enough for her to turn around to face him, preferring to hear the truth head on. His eyes firmly held hers. "Lesley Walker."

The name slid over the surface of Molly's memory and caught. "The architect?"

"We worked together a good deal over the past year."

She nodded. Other than the name, Molly had no clear picture of the woman. "She must be very special." Otherwise Jordan wouldn't love her.

"Damn it all to hell," Jordan exploded, his one good fist clenched in a tight knot at his side. "You don't need to be so damned understanding. I should have told you up front. Instead I left you hanging, thinking there might be a chance for us, when there isn't. You have every right to be angry. Throw something," he shouted, reaching for an empty vase, "you'll feel better."

She smiled and shrugged her shoulders. "You mean, you'll feel better." She removed the vase from his hand and set it back down. "Don't look so concerned. I was the one who walked out on you, remember?" Her hand trembled slightly as she opened the front door. "Whatever arrangements you make are fine. Just let me know when you need me to sign the papers."

Jordan would rather have taken another bullet than have Molly look at him the way she had when he'd announced he wanted a divorce. First her eyes had widened, as she dealt with the shock his words inflicted, then they'd gone dull and empty. It was all he could do not to reach for her with his one good arm and comfort her.

He never meant to tell her about Lesley like that, hurling the words at her without warning. He'd wanted to sit down and explain that he hadn't intended on falling in love again. It had happened. But his good intentions had taken a greased track straight to hell.

Following the doctor's instruction to sit at home and rest lasted all of an hour. He needed to get down to the job site. He needed to talk to Paul. He needed to escape his own thoughts before he questioned what he was doing. What he really needed, Jordan decided, was to have his head examined.

Lesley caught up with him at the job site. He'd been back nearly twenty-four hours before he thought to contact her. Blaming Molly for that seemed the appropriate thing to do, but he couldn't honestly do so. At the moment he wasn't keen on seeing any woman, even Lesley.

"I can't believe you're working," she said, stepping into the construction trailer, looking as wholesome and sunny as a spring day. Her eyes lit up with concern when she saw his arm in the sling. "I went to the house first. Shouldn't you be in a hospital or something?"

"Probably," Jordan muttered, allowing her to kiss his cheek.

Paul took one look at him and made a convenient excuse to leave. Jordan didn't need to ask his friend's opinion; it was there for him to read in Paul's eyes.

Jordan didn't need his best friend in order to feel guilty. After the morning confrontation with Molly, no one could make him feel more of a heel than he already did. If someone gave out awards for jackasses, he'd win first place, hands down.

"How did everything go in Manukua?" Lesley asked.

"Great."

"Molly wasn't hurt?"

"No." He made his responses brief, hoping she'd quickly realize he wasn't in the mood to talk.

"How did you feel seeing her? I mean, it's been a long time, certainly you must have felt something."

"I did."

The pain in his shoulder increased and he slumped into a chair and closed his eyes until the worst of it had passed.

"Jordan, are you all right?" Lesley pleaded. "When you phoned, you said it was nothing. You've been badly injured."

"It's little more than a flesh wound." Another understatement, but he didn't want her gushing sympathy all over him. She'd make him sound like some hero, and he wasn't.

"How long will you have to wear the sling?"

"As long as it takes," he answered shortly.

If he wasn't in such a crappy mood, he'd appreciate what a beautiful woman Lesley was. He wasn't likely to meet another like her. She understood his need for work and was ambitious herself. They were a perfect match. An ideal couple. It was time to cut the ties that bound him to Molly. Past time.

"I realize this probably isn't a good time to ask this, but did you get a chance to mention the divorce to Molly?"

Talk of the divorce left an ugly taste in his mouth. He ignored the question, stood and pretended to be involved in the blueprints.

"Naturally you didn't get a chance to talk to her, not with the country involved in a revolution," Lesley said, answering her own question. "You were lucky to get out with your lives."

"I talked to her about it this morning," he told her impatiently. "She's agreed. There won't be any problem."

Lesley went still. "I know this was difficult for you, Jordan."

She hadn't a clue, but surprisingly neither had he. A divorce seemed the natural progression for him and Molly. It was the right thing to do, but Jordan hadn't anticipated the bad feelings that came over him when he announced he formally intended to end their marriage.

"Are you having second thoughts?"

Lesley had a way of reading him that was sometimes intimidating. Was he? "No," he said without pause. The time for second thoughts was long gone. "I want the divorce," he assured her.

Larry Rife wasn't keen on divorce cases. He took them on occasionally, but generally only for a change of pace. He'd met with Jordan Larabee three or four times now and his client had assured him this was a friendly divorce. There was no such animal, but Larry didn't see the point of saying so. Larabee and his wife would discover that soon enough on their own, he suspected.

From what Larry understood, Mrs. Larabee had yet to retain her own attorney, and had indicated she saw no need to do so. Apparently she'd read over the agreement he'd drawn up and was satisfied with the settlement offer her husband had proposed.

That of its own was highly unusual, but then little about this divorce was normal. Larabee had bent over backward to make this as simple and easy for his wife as possible. Frankly, Larry couldn't help being curious what had gone wrong in their marriage.

His intercom beeped, and his secretary said, "The Larabees are here to see you."

Larry stood when the couple entered. He exchanged a courtesy handshake with Jordan, and everyone was seated. Larry couldn't help being curious about Larabee's wife. She was a pretty thing, young and fragile looking. But then appearances were often deceiving. A delicate woman wouldn't have spent the past two years as a nurse in Manukua.

Larry reached for the file and addressed the question to Molly. "Have you had the opportunity to read over the settlement offer?"

"Yes, I have," she answered in a thin voice. "And I found Jordan to be more than generous."

"It's highly unusual for you not to have an attorney look this over on your behalf," Larry felt obliged to explain. He wasn't entirely comfortable with this aspect of the divorce. It wasn't necessary, of course, but he had a certain responsibility to her.

"I don't see why. There's nothing here I take exception to, and I can see no reason to prolong the proceedings."

"As long as you understand the terms of the settlement."

"Everything is perfectly clear to me."

Larabee was unusually quiet. "He's right, Molly. It might be a good idea if you had your own attorney look it over."

"If that's what you want, but I don't see why I should. You want your freedom. You've waited long enough."

Larabee crossed his legs in what seemed a nervous movement. "I don't want you to feel that I've cheated you in any way."

"That's the last thing I need worry about with you. You've been overly generous. Why don't we leave matters as they are?"

"You're sure?"

"Positive."

She was so serene about this. Larry couldn't remember any couple who were so caring about each other over the details of a divorce. He flipped through the file for some clue of what had gone so wrong between two decent people.

"There are no children involved," he muttered to himself.

"No children," Jordan answered, although it hadn't been poised as a question.

"There was a child," Mrs. Larabee added, and Larry swore the color of her eyes changed when she spoke. When she walked in the door, he'd been struck by their clear shade of blue, but when she mentioned the child, they darkened to stormy pale agony. "A son ... he died of SIDS. His name was Jeffrey."

Jordan said nothing

Larry made a notation in the file. It was all coming together for him now. The divorce wasn't based on the usual grounds. It was rooted in grief. The pain of their loss was less when they were apart because then they could pretend to forget.

"Did you need me to sign something?" Molly Larabee asked, breaking into his thoughts. She sounded eager now, wanting this over as quickly as possible.

"Yes, of course." Larry took out the papers and then handed her a pen. "I'll file these papers this afternoon. The divorce will be final in sixty days."

"That soon?" Jordan asked.

"That long?" was his wife's question.

Larry studied the couple sitting across from him. Over the years he'd seen far too many divorces where the couple literally hated each other by the time they filed the final papers. It was disconcerting to represent two people who continued to deeply love each other.

Sitting beneath the weeping willow tree seemed the appropriate thing to do after the meeting with the attorney. Molly hadn't anticipated the emotional toll the appointment would take on her. She was grateful her father was away for the afternoon, because she needed this time alone to sort through her emotions.

She expected tears. None came. How could she weep for a marriage that had been dead all these years?

The spindly limbs of the weeping willow danced in the wind about her feet. With her back braced against the tree trunk, she stared at the meticulously kept gardens that had been her mother's pride and joy. But her mother, like Jeff, like her marriage, was dead and forever gone.

In the week since Jordan had delivered the news, Molly had made discreet inquiries about Lesley Walker. Everything she learned about the other woman was positive. Lesley was a talented architect with a promising future. She was young, energetic and well liked. As difficult as it was for Molly to stomach, Lesley was exactly the type of wife Jordan needed.

Admitting that produced a sharp pain. A knot formed in her throat and the tears that had been bottled up inside her rolled freely down her face.

"I wondered if this was where I'd find you." Her father's voice sounded from behind her.

Molly hastily wiped the moisture from her face. "I thought you were going to be away for the afternoon."

"I was," Ian Houghton said, awkwardly sitting down on the grass next to her. He looked out of place in his expensive Italian-made suit. "But I got to thinking you might be feeling a little blue after signing the final papers."

"I'm fine."

Ian handed her his crisp white handkerchief. "So I noticed." He placed his arm around her shoulders and rested his chin on the top of her head. "You used to come here when you were a little girl. The gardener's been telling me for years I should have this old tree removed, but I could never find it in my heart to do it, knowing how much you love it."

"I'm glad you didn't."

"Things aren't as bleak as they seem, sweetheart. Someday you'll look back on all this and the pain won't be nearly as deep."

Her father had said something similar after Jeff died and she hadn't found that to be true. The ache would never leave her.

"Would you rather Jordan had never been a part of your life?" Ian asked.

Her first instinct was to tell him yes, she wished she'd never met Jordan, never loved him, never given birth to his son. But it would have been a lie. Jordan was her first love, her only love, and how could she ever regret having had Jeff? It wasn't in her to lie, even to herself.

She'd failed Jordan, Molly realized, and he'd failed her. They'd been equal partners in the destruction of their marriage.

He was the first one to recognize and act on the truth. He was the first one to step out and make a new life for himself. He'd always been stronger than she was.

"I remember when Jeff died," her father said with some difficulty. It was hard for him to talk about his only grandchild. "Grief leaves one feeling hopeless. It turns you hollow inside and makes you wonder about God."

Molly was well acquainted with the toll grief demanded. "Whenever I'm hurting that badly I ask myself why God doesn't do something," she added.

"He does, but we're in too much pain to realize it."

Molly knew that, as well.

Now, nearly four years after losing their son, Jordan was moving ahead and she needed to take that first tentative step herself. "I'm going to find myself an apartment," she announced with newfound commitment.

"There's no rush," Ian was quick to tell her.

"It's time I got on with my life."

"Like Jordan?" her father questioned.

"He's right, Dad. I shouldn't have buried my pain. Heaven only knows how long I would have stayed in Manukua if it hadn't been for the revolution. I was hiding from life and, you know, it got to be downright comfortable."

"I realize I'm being selfish, but I hate to see you move out so soon."

Molly hugged her father, grateful for his love and support. He was all she had left in the world now. It was the same way it'd been from the time she was eleven, just the two of them.

Once Molly made up her mind what she was going to do, it didn't take her more than a week to find a job and an apartment. She moved several pieces of furniture from Jordan's, along with a number of personal items.

She made sure she stopped over at the house when there wasn't any chance of her running into him. For courtesy's sake, she left him notes, listing what she'd taken. She also gave him her new address.

The duplex she'd rented was in a friendly neighborhood and offered her a small yard. Molly enjoyed roses and was looking forward to planting several varieties once she was completely settled.

The apartment was roomy with two large bedrooms, a nice size kitchen and a comfortable living room. It wasn't home yet, but it would be once she had everything arranged the way she wanted. Compared to her quarters in Manukua, the duplex was a mansion. The best part about her new home was that she wasn't far from Lake Michigan and her work at Sinai Hospital.

Molly was dressed in cutoffs and a sleeveless T-shirt, placing books inside the bookcase, when the doorbell rang. She wiped the perspiration from her brow with the back of her arm and stood.

A dizzy sensation sent the room into an awkward tailspin and she collapsed onto the sofa, taking in deep, even breaths. A moment passed before the world righted itself once more.

The doorbell chimed a second time, with short, impatient bursts. No one she knew rang a bell like that except Jordan Larabee.

Standing, she composed herself as best she could and opened the front door. He had a box braced against the side of the duplex, holding it beneath his one good arm and having difficulty doing so. "It took you long enough," he complained gruffly.

"Sorry," she said, opening the screen door and stepping aside. Jordan walked in and literally dropped the box down on the carpet next to the one she was unloading into the bookcase.

"You forgot this," he said.

The dizziness returned and Molly slumped onto the arm of the sofa and pressed her hands against her face, waiting for the whirling sensation to taper.

"Are you all right?" Jordan demanded, and his brow folded in half with his concern. "You're as pale as a sheet."

"I...don't know. I must have gotten up too quickly. Everything started to spin there for a minute...I'm fine now."

"You're sure?"

"Listen, Jordan, I'm a registered nurse. I may not know a lot about some things, but I do know when I'm healthy and I tell you I'm fine."

"Good." He stuffed his hand in his pants pocket and walked around the room, surveying the duplex. "What does Ian think about all this?"

"My moving? Well, he'd rather I stayed with him the rest of my life, but I'd prefer living on my own." She surveyed the contents of what he'd brought and didn't find anything that warranted his visit. She would have picked it up the following day, or whenever she made her next trip over to the house.

Jordan strolled into the kitchen. "Do you mind if I get myself something to drink?"

"Sure." Apparently there was something more on his mind than helping her move, otherwise he wouldn't be making excuses to stay. "There's lemonade in the refrigerator. I'm afraid I don't have anything stronger."

"Lemonade's fine." He brought down a glass from the cupboard. It was a beautiful crystal one they'd received as a wedding gift from her Aunt Thelma a thousand years earlier. He paused, his hand cupped around the base of the glass.

Molly folded her hands together and moved one step forward. "I hope you don't mind that I took those glasses . . . they weren't specifically listed in the agreement. I didn't think it'd matter."

"Why should I care about a few glasses?"

"You looked as if you might object."

"I don't," he admitted gruffly. "I was just thinking about the last time we used them . . . Christmas, wasn't it?" he stopped abruptly and shook his head. "Never mind, it isn't important." Taking the glass with him, he moved into the living room and sat down on the sofa, balancing his ankle across the top of his knee. He stretched his arm out across the sofa top and appeared to be at ease.

Molly felt anything but relaxed. She sat on the ottoman opposite him, her hands pressed between her knees, waiting. Clearly there was something on his mind, something he wasn't having an easy time saying.

He took a sip of the lemonade. "How have you been?"

"Fine, and you?"

"I can't complain."

"How's the arm?"

The sling moved against his chest. "It's getting better every day. I should be able to get rid of this thing by the end of the month."

"Good."

Silence.

Molly had forgotten how loud silence could be between two people. It rang in her ears until she would have welcomed earplugs.

Briefly she wondered how long it would take him to get to the meat of the conversation, to break down and tell her what he intended.

"Was there some reason you wanted to talk to me?" she asked when she couldn't tolerate the quiet a second longer. It angered her that she had to be the one to press the issue.

He dropped his leg and leaned forward, bracing his good arm against his elbow. "The divorce will be final within the next couple of weeks."

Molly didn't need him to tell her that. "So?" She didn't mean to sound flippant, but she didn't understand his point, if he was making one.

"Are you happy?" He rubbed a hand down his face, as if he wanted to start over again and didn't know where to begin. "Damn, I'm making a mess of this. Listen," he said and vaulted to his feet. Jordan had never been able to sit in one place when something was troubling him.

"You want to know if I'm happy?" she asked, wanting to help. "Do you mean am I happy about the divorce?"

"Hell, I don't know what I want you to tell me. I have this incredible sense of guilt over God knows what. Coming here like this doesn't make a damn bit of sense, but something inside me isn't comfortable ending our marriage without...without what?" He answered his own question with another, clearly confused.

Jordan turned and their eyes met. She read his bewilderment and knew she'd experienced those same feelings herself, and like him, had been unable to put them into words.

"I guess in some ways I'm looking for you to absolve me," he said with a short, mocking laugh. "The problem is I don't know what it is I want you to forgive."

"The divorce makes me incredibly sad," she admitted in a whisper. "I don't blame you, Jordan, and I'm not angry with you if that's what you're thinking."

"Maybe you should be. Did you ever think of that?"

Molly took a moment to carefully examine her feelings. She wasn't angry now, but that didn't mean she wouldn't be in the future. All the emotions tied into the divorce and their time together in Manukua hadn't been fully processed.

"Give me time," she suggested with a weak smile.

"There's something you should know," Jordan said, and his shoulders heaved as if this was difficult for him to admit. "Lesley and I have never been lovers."

"Jordan, please, that's none of my business." She stood and walked over to the bookcase, examining the even spines of the volumes she'd recently placed inside.

"I know that. The fact is, it embarrasses the hell out of me to be talking to you about my relationship with another woman. God knows I've committed my share of sins, but adultery isn't one of them."

Their conversation was growing decidedly uncomfortable. "You asked me if I was happy," she said, throwing his question back at him. "That's what you really came to find out, and I'll tell you." She brushed the hair away from her face and held it there. "I'm ready to resume my life. I'm completely on my own for the first time . . . Africa didn't count. I have a new job I start first thing Monday morning. Am I happy? Yes, I suppose I am, but I'm not sure what happy means anymore. I haven't known since Jeff died."

Jordan's jawline went white. He seemed to need some time to compose himself. "Why is it every conversation we have boils down to Jeff?"

"He was our son."

"He's dead," Jordan shouted.

"That's the problem in a nutshell," she shouted back, and her voice trembled so badly she wondered if he'd been able to understand her. "You want to pretend Jeff never lived. You wanted to destroy his pictures and ignore the fact we had a child. I can't do that. I'll never be able to do that. Jeff was a part of you and a part of me and I refuse to deny he lived." She was sobbing now and made no effort to disguise her tears.

"How long will it take for you to forget?" Jordan demanded furiously. "Five years? Ten? When will it ever end? Tell me."

His words exploded like firecrackers dropped into the middle of the room.

"How long will you continue to grieve?"

Squaring her shoulders, Molly met his angry glare, her fists knotted at her side.

"When are you going to start? When will you stop denying we had a son? When will you be willing to own up to the fact Jeff lived?"

Jordan didn't answer, not that she expected he would. He headed for the door and nearly removed it from its hinges as he stalked outside.

Molly was trembling so much she had to sit down. She pressed her hand over her mouth to hold back the anguish that threatened to swallow her. Her stomach cramped and she knew she was going to lose her lunch. She barely made it into the bathroom in time.

Her queasy stomach didn't go away. The following morning, she woke with a headache and had to force herself out of bed. By noon she felt a little better, well enough to meet her father for lunch.

She arrived at the restaurant to find him seated and waiting for her.

"Molly, sweetheart, I'm so pleased you're feeling better. Is it the flu?"

"No," she said, wrinkling up her nose. She reached for the menu. "It's Jordan. We argued and, well, it left me terribly upset. I'm fine now."

"What did Jordan say that troubled you so much?"

"Dad," Molly chided, loving the way his voice rose with indignation as if he were ready and willing to make her husband pay handsomely for distressing her. "It's over and forgotten. The divorce will be final soon and then we'll never need have anything to do with each other again." She made a pretense of studying the menu.

The waiter arrived before she could make her selection. Her father however had already made up his mind. "I'll have a bowl of the French onion soup," he said, spreading the napkin across his lap.

The waiter looked to her expectantly. Molly's stomach heaved and she placed her hand to her abdomen at the unexpected tumult. "I'll ... I'll have a salad ... spinach salad." Her voice trembled and a paralyzing kind of numbness settled over her. She closed her eyes. There'd only been one other time that the mere mention of French onion soup had made her instantly ill.

"Molly?" Her father's concerned voice sounded as if it came from a long way off. "Is something wrong?"

She managed a weak nod. "Something's very wrong. Oh, Dad, I don't know what I'm going to do." Tears flooded her eyes and she hid her face in her hands.

"Sweetheart, tell me." He gently patted her forearm.

When she could, Molly lowered her hands away from her face. "I'm ... pregnant."

Chapter Five

Dr. Doug Anderson walked into the cubical, reading Molly's chart. Her gaze scrutinized him carefully, although she already knew the answer. She was pregnant. Not a shred of doubt lingered in her mind. When she was first pregnant with Jeff, she'd suffered the same symptoms. The bouts of morning sickness and the decreased appetite were signs she could reason away, but not the sudden and violent aversion to French onion soup.

"Well, Molly," Doug Anderson said cheerfully, smiling at her. "Congratulations are in order. Your test is positive."

"I guessed as much." She looked away, fighting down the flood of emotions. Tears were close to the surface along with the almost irresistible urge to laugh. She had an incredibly awkward sense of timing. Each emotion was foreshadowed with a growing sense of fear.

"Molly, are you all right?"

She gestured with her hands, not knowing how to answer him. "I'm afraid, Doug, more afraid than I can ever remember being." She'd lost her son; she didn't know if she could bear to relive the nightmare a second time.

Doug pulled out a chair and sat down. "You aren't going to lose this baby to SIDS," he said, sounding remarkably confident.

"You can't guarantee that." She was a medical professional herself and knew the statistics well. Crib death is the major cause of infant death in the United States. She didn't need anyone to tell her that one out of every five hundred babies dies mysteriously, for no apparent cause. She was also aware that the chance of losing a second child to SIDS was so infinitesimally small that it shouldn't warrant her concern. But it did.

How could she not worry? It wasn't humanly possible.

"It's more than that," she whispered, fighting hard to keep her voice from shaking. "Jordan and I are divorcing. It'll be final soon."

Doug looked as if he wasn't sure what to say. "I didn't know."

Molly didn't want to rehash her marital troubles, especially with someone who was familiar with Jordan. "I realize I'll need to tell him about the baby." The prospect filled her with a deepening sense of dread. An uneasiness settled on her like an anchor hitting the bottom of the sea.

"He'll want to know," her physician added. "It could make a difference."

Molly agreed with a nod. Doug seemed to think the news might have some effect on the divorce proceedings, but Molly sincerely doubted that. Jordan was involved with Lesley. He was the one who wanted out of the marriage. Oh dear heaven, this complicated everything.

Doug gently patted her hand and asked, "Is there anything I can do for you?"

"No, but thanks for asking."

"I'd like you to make an appointment in two weeks."

"All right," she said, knowing she sounded like a robot. That was the way she felt, as if the simplest movements demanded a major effort.

Molly didn't know how much time passed after Doug left the cubical and she found the energy to move. Although a part of her had accepted the information that she was indeed pregnant, another equally strong part of her had dallied in the comfort of denial. That luxury had been taken away from her. She was carrying Jordan's child. Soon her womb would stretch and fill to accommodate this new life they'd created.

Naturally she had no option but to tell Jordan. The task, however, held no appeal.

She returned to her apartment, changed into shorts and a sleeveless top, poured herself a glass of iced tea and sank into her chaise longue on her sunlit patio. She needed to review her options. Getting in touch with her emotions proved difficult. She couldn't seem to get past the nearly suffocating fear of losing a second child.

She'd barely had time to assimilate all the changes a baby would bring into her life when the doorbell chimed, scattering her thoughts like marbles against a hardwood floor.

She opened the front door to find Jordan, dressed as if he'd recently walked off the job site, still wearing his hard hat. He wore a frown as if he were displeased about something.

"Hello, Jordan." For one wild moment, her heart went into a panic, fearing that he'd somehow learned about the pregnancy. It didn't take her that long to realize he wouldn't be nearly this calm if that were the case.

"Do you mind if I come in for a moment?" he asked.

"Please." She held open the screen door for him, all the while wondering at the purpose of his visit. If they were to make the break, she'd rather it was clean. Having him repeatedly pop in unannounced didn't sit well. Apparently it didn't with him, either, because he looked about as comfortable as a voodoo doctor in a Methodist prayer meeting.

"Would you like a glass of iced tea?" she asked. He looked tempted, then shook his head.

"Listen, I thought I should clear something with you."

"About what?"

"Kati's wedding."

Her cousin's wedding was scheduled for that Saturday.

"She sent me an invitation," Jordan went on to say. "I'm fond of Kati and, frankly, I'd like to go. But I won't. Not if it'll be awkward for you."

"Jordan, for heaven's sake, don't be ridiculous. Of course you should go. Kati's been half in love with you for years. There isn't any reason why you shouldn't go."

He rubbed his forearm across his brow and lowered his gaze. "I was thinking about asking Lesley to join me."

The other woman's name pricked at her pride, but Molly would have rather walked across a bed of hot coals than let Jordan know. "Are you asking my permission?"

"In a way, yes," he said, which was a concession coming from him.

"We're getting divorced, remember?"

"I'm trying to be as up front with you as possible," Jordan said, his voice elevated as though he were struggling to maintain his composure. "The situation might be awkward and it seemed only fair to give you notice."

"My family will find out about the divorce eventually. Now is as good a time as any to get it out in the open."

"If you'd rather I didn't invite Lesley, then . . ."

"Jordan, please, you've got to make that decision yourself. Don't ask me to do it for you."

"I don't want the wedding to be uncomfortable for you."

"Stop worrying about me."

"It's your family."

"Do you think the divorce will come as a shock to my relatives?" she asked, forcing a short laugh. "We've been separated for three years."

He nodded, but he wasn't happy with what she'd had to say. It came to her that she should tell him about the baby right then and be done with it. The sooner she let him know, the better it would be for everyone involved.

Jordan walked over to the front door, his hand on the knob. "I'll see you Saturday afternoon, then."

"Jordan." His name had a frantic edge to it and he turned around immediately.

"Yes."

She looked at him, debating if she should tell him about the baby and instinctively knew she couldn't. Not yet. She needed time to come to grips with the news herself before she confronted him. When she told Jordan, she'd need to be strong and confident, and right then she was neither.

"Nothing," she said, offering him an apologetic smile. "I'll see you Saturday."

Jordan was fond of Kati. She was by far his favorite of Molly's cousins, and since she'd specifically sent him a wedding invitation he felt honor bound to attend the gala event.

There was more to his determination to attend this family function than sharing in Kati's happiness, Jordan was forced to admit.

True, this wedding was an excellent means of broadcasting his divorce from Molly. He would use this social event to introduce the woman he intended on marrying, but there was more to it than that. It was his way of proving to himself that the marriage, the relationship, was completely over, completely dead.

Inviting Lesley had been a calculated risk on his part and Jordan had heavily weighed the decision. If he attended the wedding alone, it was a foregone conclusion that one or more of Molly's aunts would take it upon themselves to speak to him and possibly Molly about the breakup of their marriage.

By bringing Lesley with him, he was making a statement to all those concerned that the divorce was imminent. Any well-meaning advice at this late date would be lost on him and Molly.

The decision made, he picked up Lesley, who he swore never looked better. She was a lovely woman and she deeply cared for him. They would make a good life together. Jordan didn't know why he found it necessary to remind himself of that so often. He'd be glad when this divorce business was over and done with. He found the whole process distasteful.

For some unknown reason, he couldn't make himself stop feeling guilty. Hell if he knew what he had to feel guilty about. Molly was the one who'd abandoned him. She'd been away three long years.

All right, so he'd made an ass of himself in Manukua, but given the circumstances, that was forgivable. As for the divorce, he'd bent over backward to be fair in his settlement offer. More than fair. All he was asking for was his freedom. There wasn't a reason in hell he should feel the way he did.

"You're looking thoughtful," Lesley commented as they drove to the church.

Lesley often sensed his mood. She knew him well. He reached over and squeezed her hand. "I was just doing a little thinking."

"About what?"

"Our own wedding," he lied, and the words nearly caught in his throat. "We should start making the arrangements soon, don't you think?"

Her hesitation surprised him. "I'm not in any rush and I don't think you should be, either."

"Why not?"

"Jordan, a divorce takes time."

"Four lousy weeks!"

"I don't mean legally, I mean personally. You're going to need to grieve the loss of your marriage before we can start making any wedding plans ourselves."

"Grieve the marriage," he repeated impatiently. What did she think he'd been doing the past three years. There was nothing left to mourn. It was dead, and he had no intention of digging it up and examining it all over again.

"You'll understand more once it's final," Lesley added with a soft sigh.

He didn't know what had made her such an expert on the subject and bit his tongue to keep from saying so. The last thing he wanted to do was argue, especially now.

"Fine, whatever you say," he muttered as they approached the church.

Finding a parking place proved to be a bear, and his mood hadn't improved by the time the ushers seated them on the bride's side of the church. The first person he saw, two rows up from him and Lesley, was Molly. She was wearing a pretty outfit with a red blazer and a pleated red-and-white flowered skirt. He remembered the suit from years earlier and how she'd struggled to fit back into it after Jeff had been born. It fit her just fine now. Just fine.

Thankfully they didn't need to wait long before the organ music filled the sanctuary and the bridesmaids ceremonially marched down the center aisle. Jordan stood with the others when Kati approached on her father's arm.

Uncomfortable emotions began to stir awake memories of his and Molly's wedding. Dear sweet heaven, they'd been so deeply in love. They were young, younger than they should have been, and crazy about each other.

Jordan vividly recalled when Ian had escorted Molly down the same church aisle and how he'd stood at the front of the altar waiting for her, thinking he'd never seen a more beautiful woman in his life. He remembered the vows he'd spoken that day and how his voice had wobbled with the intensity of what he was feeling. He'd meant every word.

Molly had looked up at him, her eyes filled with devotion as she'd repeated her own vows. Jordan could remember thinking he'd rather die than stop loving her.

The years hadn't changed that. He did love Molly. Not in the same way he had the day they'd married. He'd been little more than wet behind the ears. Over time his love had matured and grown. He remembered when Jeff was born...

His thoughts came to a slow, grinding halt, and he gave himself a mental shake, refusing to drag his son into this.

Everyone sat back down and Jordan was grateful. Not because standing had become a burden, but the change gave him the opportunity to focus his attention on the bride and groom and push the memories of his own long-ago wedding to the farthest corner of his mind.

That, however, proved to be impossible. Kati and Matt seemed intent on everyone joining them as they exchanged their vows. Lesley reached for his hand, and for the briefest of moments he was surprised to realize she was with him. It shocked him to look down and find another woman other than Molly standing at his side. To his credit, he recovered quickly.

Jordan tucked Lesley's hand around his elbow and patted it, hoping to reassure her of his devotion. He did care for her, but he didn't love her, not with the magnitude with which he'd loved Molly.

He didn't appreciate the track down which his thoughts were leading him. Of course he loved Molly, he reassured himself. They'd been married—and would be for another four weeks. They shared a history together. What Lesley had said earlier about needing to grieve their marriage made sense. He wasn't sure he needed to wear sackcloth and ashes, but a certain adjustment in thinking would be necessary.

Before he realized what was happening, Kati and Matt were involved in a deep kiss to the approval of their guests. Smiling, the two hurried down the aisle together, arm in arm, their happiness glowing as bright as the noonday sun. Molly and he had been that happy once, a long time ago.

The reception was held at the country club, the very same one where he and Molly had held their own wedding reception. Jordan hadn't made the connection until they arrived. He wished now that he'd mailed Kati her gift and left it at that.

The valet parked his car, and Jordan and Lesley walked through the clubhouse and onto the lush green grass where the dinner and dance were being held. The yard was beautifully decorated with Chinese lanterns and round tables and white wooden chairs. The food was exquisitely displayed on long linen-covered tables beneath the white canopies.

By then he was beginning to have second thoughts about the wisdom of following through with this. He decided to drop off his gift, congratulate the new-lyweds, make his excuses and leave.

"Jordan Larabee, my goodness, is that you?"

He found himself face-to-face with Molly's Aunt Johanna. He loved her dearly, but the woman was a born meddler. "Aunt Johanna," he said, hugging her briefly. When he finished, he placed his arm around Lesley's shoulders. "I'd like to introduce you to Lesley Walker, my fiancée."

Aunt Johanna giggled as if she'd heard a joke. "How can you be engaged when you're married to Molly? Why that's downright amusing. You'd think it was April Fool's Day instead of May."

Jordan wished he'd thought to warn Lesley. "Molly and I are divorcing," he explained. "And I've asked Lesley to be my wife."

Aunt Johanna's face turned a bright shade of pink. "Oh, Jordan, I'm so very sorry to hear that. I mean it's sad for Molly, but good for... oh, dear," she said, pressing her hands to her face. "I seem to be making a mess of this."

"There's no need to apologize," Lesley said, her natural graciousness taking over. "It was an honest mistake."

Jordan was grateful by how well she handled the uncomfortable scene.

"It was good to see you again," Molly's aunt said, making a hasty exit.

"I'm sorry," Jordan whispered. And he was. He should have warned her about what to expect and wanted to kick himself for being so insensitive to her feelings.

"Jordan, it wasn't that big a deal."

"We'll make our excuses and leave."

Lesley placed her hand on his arm. "We most certainly will not. Leaving now will embarrass poor Aunt Johanna and leave Molly to make lengthy explanations. The last thing she needs is to explain what you were doing here with another woman."

Lesley was right. "We'll stay no more than an hour, though, agreed?"

"Perfect," Lesley said, brightly smiling up at him. "It's going to be all right, darling, I promise."

Lesley wasn't one to use affectionate terms and having her do so now came as something of a surprise. It wasn't until later that he realized she was staking her claim on her territory. That pleased him. Lesley wasn't immune to a few pangs of jealousy.

Jordan was even more surprised to realize he wasn't exempt from being visited by the green-eyed monster himself. Only the source was Molly. Once the meal was served by waiters in white jackets, the band struck up and the space was cleared for dancing.

Jordan had originally intended to stay for the first few dances, the traditional ones between the bride and groom, but before he knew it he was on the dance floor, enjoying himself with Lesley.

He couldn't remember the last time he'd let go like this. It surprised him to realize how good it felt to throw back his head and laugh.

Then he saw Molly, dancing.

The sight of her in the arms of another man had a curious effect upon him. He felt like he'd been slapped alongside of the head. The mental punch was powerful enough to leave his ears ringing.

He didn't give any outward indication of what he experienced, although he made an excuse to leave the dance floor soon afterward.

"Don't tell me you're tired already," Lesley complained. "We were just getting started."

"I need something to drink," Jordan said, reaching for a champagne glass from a waiter's tray as he walked past. He preferred red wine to bubbly champagne, but it was any port in a storm and he felt as if he'd been hit by hurricane-force winds.

It took some doing to divert his gaze away from Molly and her partner, and focus his attention on Lesley instead. He didn't recognize the tall, good-looking man with his soon-to-be ex-wife. He held her in a possessive way that tightened Jordan's jaw.

Thankfully there were plenty of acquaintances to renew, plenty of people to occupy himself with until he decided what he was going to do. If anything.

Carrying his champagne glass with him, Jordan circulated the area, introducing Lesley and doing his damnedest to ignore the fact his wife was in the arms of another man.

"Hello, Jordan, it's good to see you."

"Ian," Jordan said, courteously inclining his head. "Have you met Lesley Walker?"

"Hello, Lesley," Ian said, taking her hand and raising it to his lips. His father-in-law had always been a consummate charmer, and within a relatively short while had Lesley eating out of his palm.

Lesley must have guessed that Ian had something private he wanted to say because she mumbled something about powdering her nose and quietly slipped away.

"You're looking good," Ian said and slapped him across the back. "Back to a hundred per cent after your little adventure, I see."

Jordan frowned. "I'm fine. Get to it, Ian."

"Get to it?" The old man did a fair job of pretending.

"Say what it is you want and be done with it," Jordan advised.

Ian looked downright amused. His eyes were bright with a touch of irony as if it was all he could do not to laugh outright. "I don't have anything important to say," Ian murmured, but the edges of his mouth quivered. "That might not be the case with my daughter, however. When was the last time you talked to her?"

"This week, why?"

"Why?" Ian said, breaking into a ready smile. "You'll need to ask her that."

"I will." This was just the excuse Jordan had been looking for. He set his champagne glass aside and walked onto the dance floor. Molly's eyes widened with surprise when he tapped her partner on the shoulder. "I'm cutting in," he said without apology and a sorry lack of manners. And proceeded to do exactly that.

"Jordan," she said, staring up at him, "that was downright rude."

He didn't have a word to say in his defense, so he let the comment drop. "What's your father grinning ear to ear about?" he demanded.

Molly's gaze darted away from his. "Nothing," she answered smoothly. "You know my how my dad gets this way sometimes. If . . . he's troubling you, I'll be happy to say something to him."

She did a commendable job of disguising whatever it was she was feeling. Jordan might have believed her if he hadn't felt her stiffen in his arms the moment he mentioned Ian.

"Tell me."

"There's nothing to tell."

"You're sure?"

"What could I possibly have to say at this late date?"

She felt damn good there, in his embrace, and after a little while he forgot why he'd asked her to dance and enjoyed the simple pleasure of holding her.

"It was a beautiful wedding," he said as means of carrying the conversation.

"It reminded me a little of our own." He knew the minute she admitted that, Molly regretted it. "The comparison is inevitable really. The same church...our reception was held here, too, remember? We were about the same ages, too, and we invited so many of the same guests."

"Don't worry, I know what you're saying." It made sense she'd noticed the same things he had. The same brooding emotions.

Jordan wondered what she'd been thinking while Kati and Matt exchanged their wedding vows. He wondered if she remembered how his voice had wobbled or how her eyes had filled with tears. Did the memory of how desperately they'd been in love come back to haunt her, as well?

"It's a beautiful wedding," she said after an awkward moment.

"Real nice," Jordan agreed.

The music stopped and he had a difficult time dropping his arms and stepping away from her.

"You'd better get back to Lesley," she whispered, lowering her gaze.

Lesley. He'd damn near forgotten her. "Yeah. Your dance partner's tossing daggers my way, as well." It was a weak attempt at a joke. A weak attempt of getting the information he wanted about the other man.

Molly was kind enough to smile. "David's not like that."

"Who is he?" Jordan asked, hoping to sound casual and approving.

"David Stern. Dr. David Stern. He works at Sinai. We met last week."

"He's your date," Jordan said, stunned by the realization. Talk about being obtuse! He hadn't noticed Stern at the church, but that was understandable. His gaze hadn't filtered past Molly in her cheery red suit and broad-rimmed white hat. It hadn't occurred to him to notice the man who was standing next to her.

"Not really," Molly was quick to tell him. "David's a family friend of Matt's. I didn't realize he knew Matt, and David didn't know Kati was my cousin. We'd both talked about attending a wedding on Saturday without realizing it was the same one."

"I see," Jordan said stiffly. He didn't like Stern. Dr. Stern, he corrected.

"Lesley looks very nice," Molly said, glancing behind him.

"Have you talked to your Aunt Johanna lately?" Jordan said as they walked off the dance floor. He was making excuses to linger and knew it, although he didn't understand why he found it necessary. Nor did he want to know.

"Apparently she wasn't aware we're divorcing," Molly said, answering his unspoken question. "You needn't worry, the word will get around fast now. Aunt Johanna is the family gossip. Everyone who's even distantly related will hear the news by nightfall." Her smile was forced, but only someone who knew Molly well would see through that. "I hope she didn't embarrass you."

"No," Jordan muttered. "What about you?"

"Not in the least. It's better if people know as soon as possible, don't you think?" She seemed eager to leave now, looking around as if she were trying to locate her precious David.

"I'd better get back to Lesley," he said, making his own excuses. "It was good dancing with you again."

"You, too." How polite they sounded, as though they were little more than strangers. That was the way it would have to be, he told himself. They had no future, only a sorry, pain-filled past.

Jordan's gaze followed her as she moved across the dance floor. Instead of finding her date, she took the most direct route to her father's side. Even from this distance he could see that she was irritated with Ian. His father-in-law took her chastisement with a grain of salt, reaching for a glass of champagne halfway through her tirade.

Apparently there was something more to the lazy, I-know-something-you-don't smile Ian wore. Jordan wondered what the hell it was, but he had a sneaking suspicion he'd find out soon enough.

Monday morning Jordan got a call from Larry Rife. "I just got the court docket, and the final hearing is set for Thursday afternoon."

"That soon."

"Count your blessings," Rife went on to say. "If Molly had wanted to, she could have tied you up in court for years."

"But it hasn't been the full four weeks yet?"

His lawyer hesitated. "Are you sure you want to go through with this?"

"Yes, I'm sure," Jordan snapped. "Fine, I'll be in court on Thursday afternoon. What time?"

Larry told him. Jordan stared at the telephone receiver for a long time afterward. Thursday afternoon would be the end of his marriage. Thursday afternoon some judge he'd never seen would pound his gavel and his life with Molly would end.

He waited until he suspected she would be home from work before he dialed her phone number. She answered on the third ring; her voice was reed thin as if she were ill and struggling hard not to show it.

"It's Jordan," he announced. "What's wrong? You sound like you're sick."

"I'm fine."

She sure as hell didn't sound like it. "Have you got the flu?"

"Something like that."

He would have liked to question her more, but wasn't sure how to pursue it. "I got a call from Larry Rife this afternoon," he said, getting to the purpose of his call. He didn't relish this task. "The divorce will be final on Thursday."

"Will I need to be in court?"

"No. Not unless you want to be."

"I don't."

"I was the one who filed, I'll go. Do you want me to call you afterward?"

She hesitated as if this was a momentous decision. "That won't be necessary. Thursday it is, then. Thank you for letting me know."

It seemed crass to tell her she was welcome. Crass to thank her for the good years they'd shared. Now didn't seem the time to tell her how sorry he was about Jeff, or mention how badly he'd failed them both.

He'd assumed getting the divorce was a formality. All that was required of him was his signature. No one had told him it was like having his arms torn off and that it would leave him feeling as if he were sitting on a pile of rotting garbage. It wasn't supposed to be like this.

"Goodbye, Molly," he said after a moment.

"Goodbye, Jordan." Her voice quivered and he knew she was experiencing the same things he was. They shared the same pain, the same deep sense of loss.

From Thursday onward it would be like that song Molly sometimes sang. She'd be someone he used to love.

"Jordan," she said quickly as if she were afraid he'd already hung up the phone. Her voice rang with a note of panic.

"Yes," he said softly, reassuringly.

An eternity passed before she spoke. "Nothing."

"Molly, listen, I know we're divorcing, but if you ever need me for anything..."

"Thank you, but that won't be necessary."

"I see." He didn't have any reason to be hurt by her words, but he was.

"I didn't mean that the way it sounded," she said softly, regretfully. "Thank you for the offer, Jordan, I appreciate it. If you ever need me for anything, don't hesitate to call."

"I won't." Although he doubted that he would. "Goodbye," he said a second time and gently replaced the receiver before she could echo the sentiment.

For reasons Jordan didn't want to analyze he didn't have the heart to hear her say the words a second time.

Chapter Six

"If you don't tell Jordan before Thursday afternoon, I swear I will."

"Dad!" Molly argued, so frustrated she wanted to weep. "This is none of your business."

"I'm making it my business!" He stood and walked around his bulky desk until he stood no more than a few feet from where she was sitting. They rarely disagreed, and when they did Molly could generally reason with her father. Not this time.

"Jordan has a right to know he's going to become a father."

"I'll tell him in my own good time," Molly insisted.

"You'll tell him before Thursday," Ian pressed.

"Do you seriously believe Jordan will call off the divorce?"

"Yes."

"The baby isn't going to make any difference in how he feels about Lesley. He wants his freedom...my pregnancy isn't going to stand in his way."

"We'll see, won't we?"

Ian was serious; if she didn't tell Jordan she was pregnant, he'd take on the task himself. She almost wished she could let him. Walking over to the phone she punched out the number she knew so well. Jordan answered abruptly on the second ring.

"Are you alone?" she asked brusquely.

"Yes, why?"

"I'm coming over."

"Now?"

"Yes, I'll be there in ten minutes," she said and slapped down the receiver. Her father smiled approvingly until she walked over to the liquor cabinet and took out a full bottle of his favorite Kentucky whiskey.

"Where are you taking that?" he demanded.

"To Jordan, he's going to need it."

Her father chuckled and escorted her to the front door, opening it for her. "Give me a call later."

"You're a conniving old man."

"I know," Ian Houghton said, beaming her a wide smile. "How do you think I got to be bank president?" The sound of his amusement followed her out the front door.

By the time Molly pulled into the driveway of the home she'd once shared with Jordan, she'd changed her mind no less than three times. She might have done so again, if he hadn't immediately opened the door and stood on the porch and waited for her.

"What's going on?" he asked.

Molly didn't answer him. Instead she walked into the house and headed straight for the kitchen and brought down a thick glass tumbler. Next she walked over to the refrigerator, opened the freezer door and filled the glass with ice. She poured Jordan a stiff drink and handed it to him.

"What's that for?" he asked, frowning.

"You might want to sit down."

"What the hell's going on?"

Molly had thought she could do this unemotionally, but she was wrong. She was shaking like meadow grass stirred up by the force of high winds.

"If you won't sit down I will," she announced, slumping into a chair. She set the whiskey bottle on the table, and it made a loud clanking noise that echoed through the kitchen.

"What's gotten into you?" Jordan insisted. He pulled out the chair across from her. "I realize this divorce thing is more emotionally wrenching than either of us expected."

Her eyes started to water. "This doesn't have to do with the divorce."

"Why else are you here?"

"Oh, honestly, Jordan," she said impatiently, "don't be so obtuse."

"Obtuse? About what?"

She had an aversion to coming right out and telling him. "Think about it," she suggested, gesturing wildly with her free hand. The other continued to hold the bottle.

"I am thinking."

What she needed was a stiff drink of that whiskey herself, but she couldn't, not when she was pregnant.

"Care to join me?" Jordan asked, bringing down a second tumbler.

"It isn't a good idea for me now. Trust me, it's tempting, I could use the courage."

"It's probably better that you don't. You never could hold your liquor."

"Great, insult me."

He stared at her as if he hadn't seen her in a long while, as if studying her would tell him what it was he didn't know.

"We made love in Manukua, remember?" She waved the whiskey bottle at him, hoping to jolt his memory.

"Yeah, but why bring it up now?" As soon as the words left his lips, he made the connection, falling back into the wooden chair. Slowly his eyes linked with hers. His went wide and then narrowed as he reached for the tumbler and drank down a big gulp. He pressed the back of his hand to his mouth the same way she had and briefly closed his eyes. "You're pregnant."

"Nothing gets past you, does it?" she said mockingly.

"How long have you known?" Why he found that so important, she could only guess.

"A couple of weeks."

"It's taken you until now to tell me?"

She recognized the tone of his voice. His anger simmered just below the surface. Outwardly he was as calm and collected as the next man, but the deep, almost imperceptible inflection of his voice gave him away.

"Sure," she cried, "blame me. I didn't get pregnant all by myself, I'll have you know. Oh no, you had to come after me like Indiana Jones, sweep me into your arms and make mad, passionate love to me.''

''I didn't plan for that to happen,'' he said in his defense.

''Are you saying I did?''

''No,'' he shouted and wiped his hand down his blood-drained face. He reached for the whiskey and refilled his glass. ''What are you going to do?'' he asked, not looking at her.

''About what?''

''The pregnancy?''

''That's a stupid question to ask. I'm going to have this baby, raise him or her and live long enough to be a problem to my grandchildren. What else is there to do?''

Jordan propped his elbows against the tabletop. ''What about the divorce?''

''I don't see where this pregnancy should make any difference. Lesley will understand.'' Although Molly would have thoroughly enjoyed being a bug on the wall when he broke the news to his faithful fiancée.

''You might have said something sooner, don't you think?'' he flared. His eyes glared at her accusingly. ''You knew on Saturday, didn't you? That's what your father was hinting about. Who else did you tell—your good friend Dr. Stern?''

''Leave David out of this.''

''So it's David now instead of Dr. Stern.''

''Listen, Jordan, I've done my duty and told you about the baby. I realize it's a shock . . . it was a shock to me, too, but this needn't change anything. You can go about your merry way and do as you damn well please.''

Jordan scowled back at her. "You might have given me some warning. I don't know what the hell I'm going to do."

"Might I suggest—nothing?"

"No," he growled.

"Here," she said, handing him the whiskey bottle. "When you've had time to think this through, give me a call and we can talk this out in a more reasonable fashion."

Reasonable fashion!

It was just like Molly to waltz into his home, the night before the divorce was due to be final, and casually announce she was pregnant.

Jordan was furious. He reached for the tumbler, and the ice clanked against the sides of the glass as he jerked it toward his mouth. At least she had the foresight to realize he was going to need a good, stiff drink to help him deal with this.

Pregnant.

He had to give Molly credit. She had an incredible sense of timing. Leave it to his wife to drop a bombshell at the worst possible moment.

A baby.

Jordan's hand tightened around his drink. Sweet heaven, how could this have happened? If it wasn't so incredulous, he'd laugh. Weeping, however, seemed far more appropriate.

Molly had had time to adjust to this news. He hadn't. Frankly, he didn't know that he ever would. Dealing with the possibility of losing a second child was beyond his scope of endurance.

His hand was shaking and Jordan realized it had nothing to do with the amount of alcohol he'd consumed. He'd never been fond of whiskey, Kentucky smooth or otherwise.

He was frightened. So damn frightened he shook with it. Give him a band of machine-gun toting rebels any day of the week. Another gunshot wound was preferable to the risks involved in loving another child.

The grandfather clock in the living room signaled the time, reminding him there was only a matter of hours before he stood before a judge.

"Thank you so much for meeting with me," Amanda Clayton said when Molly joined her on the wooden bench in Lincoln Park. She was a petite thing, young with thick dark hair that naturally curled under at her shoulders.

Pierre had gifted Molly with a dozen or more croissants over the past few weeks in an effort to encourage her to meet his suffering daughter. Molly had finally agreed, but she wasn't sure she would be able to say anything that would help.

Although the day was cloudy and overcast, Amanda wore sunglasses. Molly wasn't fooled, the glasses were an effort to disguise the blotchy red eyes from the ever-ready flow of tears.

"How long has it been?" Molly asked gently.

"Christi died six months ago yesterday. How...how about you?"

"Jeff's been gone almost four years now."

"Four years," Amanda echoed, then added softly. "Does it ever get any better? Does the pain ever go away?"

"I don't know." Molly had been uncomfortable about this meeting from the first. How could she possibly help someone else when she hadn't been able to help herself? "I can get through a day without crying now," Molly told her.

"How . . . how long did that take?"

"Two years."

"What about your husband?"

"How do you mean?"

"This seems so much harder for me than it does Tommy. I can't even talk about Christi with him because he thinks we should forget, but how am I supposed to forget her?"

"You can't and you won't. You're husband's hurting, too, but men have a far more difficult time expressing their grief. My husband never cried, at least not when I could see him." She knew Jordan had grieved in his own way, but never openly and never with her.

"What . . . what did you do with Jeff's things? I know this must sound stupid, but what am I supposed to do with Christi's clothes and her toys and the special things we bought for her? Do I just pack those away as if she'd never lived? Or do I leave them out?"

"I don't know," Molly answered sadly.

"What did you do?"

Molly knotted her hands into tight fists. "A few days after we buried Jeff, my . . . husband went into our son's bedroom, closed the door and packed up all his things to give to a charitable organization."

Molly vividly remembered the terrible argument that had followed as she fanatically sorted through the boxes removing the precious items that had marked Jeff's all-too-short life. She'd managed to salvage his baby book, a hand-knit blanket and his baptismal gown. A rattle, too, and a few other things that were important to her.

Their argument had scarred their marriage. It was as though Jordan believed if he could cut out every piece of evidence that Jeff had lived, then the pain would stop. They'd each dealt with their grief in different ways. Molly had clung to every memory of Jeff. While Jordan had systematically pushed their son out of his life.

This was what had driven them apart. In looking at Molly, Jordan was forced to remember his son. In looking at Jordan, Molly was forced into dealing with Jeff's death.

"Tommy thinks we should sell the house."

"Do you want to move?" Molly asked gently.

"No. Tommy feels that there was something in the air that caused Christi to die. He believes the same thing will happen if we have another baby, but I love our home, and the neighbors have been wonderful. I don't want to move where I don't know anyone. I talked to the doctor about it and he's assured me nothing in the environment was responsible. Besides," Amanda added, "I don't have the energy it would take to find a new home and then pack up everything we own. It's all I can do to get from one day to the next."

Molly understood that, as well. For weeks after Jeff died it was all she could manage to get out of bed in the morning and dress. By contrast, Jordan was up at the crack of dawn and didn't return until long after the dinner hour.

Work had been his release, his salvation. There hadn't been any such relief for Molly, not until she realized she couldn't continue to live with Jordan.

"Eventually I went back to work," Molly said, remembering how it had taken eight long months for her to function again. "That helped me more than anything, although I don't think it was a solution. At least when I was working I didn't dwell on 'if only.'" She dragged in a deep breath, knowing only someone who'd suffered these kinds of regrets would understand. "You see, I'm a nurse, and as a medical professional I couldn't keep from blaming myself. I should have known...I should have been able to do something. Jeff woke that morning and cried. I...I wanted to catch a few minutes' extra sleep and so I stayed in bed. By the time I climbed out of bed..." It wasn't necessary to finish.

"Tommy and I woke before Christi and he wanted to go in and get her up, but I told him to let her sleep while I went in and took a shower. Only she wasn't sleeping," Amanda said, her voice cracking, "she was dead."

Molly reached for Amanda's hand and gently squeezed her fingers.

"I lost more than my baby when Christi died," Amanda whispered brokenly. "I lost my faith, too. I don't attend church services anymore. I don't want to believe in a God who allows children to die."

Molly had made her peace with God early in the grieving process. She'd felt so terribly alone and needed Him so desperately. "I can't believe God caused Jeff's death, but I know He allowed it."

Amanda reached for her purse. "Would you like to see Christi's picture?"

"Very much," Molly said.

Amanda opened her purse and handed her a small padded photo album. Christi had been a beautiful baby with a head full of dark, curly hair and bright blue eyes. "She looks like such a happy baby."

"She was. I sometimes wonder..." Amanda didn't finish. She didn't need to; Molly understood. She'd wondered herself what Jeff's life would have been like had he lived. Her own life, and Jordan's, too, would have been drastically different. It was as if the world had spun off its axis early one Saturday morning nearly four years ago.

"I have to get back to the hospital," Molly explained. They'd already talked much longer than what she'd expected.

"I'm glad we met."

"I am, too. I don't know that I helped you."

"But you have," Amanda assured her. "More than you realize. Would it be all right if we got together again sometime. I know it'd help my husband if he could talk to yours."

"I'm sorry," Molly said, struggling now to keep her voice even. It was the first time she'd ever spoken the words aloud. "Jordan and I are divorced."

"Oh, I'm so sorry."

Molly stared into the distance until she'd composed herself enough to respond. "So am I."

She should probably do something wild and expensive, Molly decided when she got off work that afternoon. It wasn't every day a woman got divorced. Surely the occasion called for a shopping spree or a lengthy appointment with a masseuse. A divorce demanded more than a hot-fudge sundae, or even a banana split.

Molly had almost reached her car when she heard someone calling her name. She turned around to find Dr. David Stern briskly walking toward her.

"Hi," he greeted breathlessly. "I was beginning to think I wasn't going to catch you."

"Hello again." She was mildly surprised he'd been looking for her. They'd danced a few times at Kati and Matt's wedding, and ate together on the lush green lawn, but she hadn't talked to him after Jordan had been so rude.

"I was hoping I could convince you to go out to dinner with me tonight," David said. He was tall and burly. A few of the staff members referred to him as Dr. Bear, not because of his temperament, but for his size.

"Tonight," she repeated.

"I realize it's short notice, but I'm on call the rest of the week. We could make it another night if that's more convenient, but it never fails. If I've got a date, someone decides this is the night they're going to hurl themselves off a cliff." His grin was wide and boyish.

Molly had liked him the moment she'd watched him comfort an elderly patient. David might be as big and burly as a bear, but he was as gentle as a newborn kitten when needed.

"I'd enjoy dinner with you very much," Molly told him. "But not tonight."

"You've got other plans?"

"In a way. My divorce was final this afternoon and, well, I was thinking I should do something...extravagant. I don't know what yet. Something reckless."

"Hey, some would say dinner with me was downright daring."

Molly was sorely tempted to accept the invitation, but she wasn't ready to date again, not so soon. In addition, there was the baby. Not every man would be thrilled to date a pregnant woman. "I don't think I'd be very good company."

"I understand," he said, and although he sounded disappointed he offered her a warm smile. "If you need to talk to someone, give me a call." He reached for his prescription pad from his jacket pocket, wrote out his home phone number, peeled off the sheet and handed it to her.

"Promise me one thing," he said, "don't sit around home alone and mope. I'll be in all evening if you want to talk. If nothing else, I've got this great joke book and I can read it to you over the phone."

Impulsively Molly hugged him. She could use a friend just now.

A few minutes later, Molly walked into her apartment and closed the door. The sun had broken through the afternoon clouds and the sky was a polished shade of blue. Funny how bright everything could be when she was weathering a fierce emotional storm. The least it could do was drizzle. A downpour would have been more appropriate.

The phone rang and Molly swerved around to look at it. Perhaps it was fanciful thinking on her part, but she half hoped it was Jordan calling to tell her how the final divorce proceedings had gone. That wasn't likely, however, and she knew it.

"Hello."

"How are you?" It was her ever-loving father.

"Fine."

"You didn't call me," he chastised her. "How did your talk go with Jordan?"

"It went. He wasn't overly pleased, as you might imagine."

"Did he change his mind about the divorce?"

"No." Some small part of her had hoped he would, although she'd never have verbalized as much to her father. Had only now admitted it to herself.

All Ian's talk had ignited a spark of hope, however futile, that her marriage could be saved. But Jordan was involved with Lesley now. It made sense that he was looking to sever his ties with her.

"You told Jordan about the baby, didn't you?"

"Yes."

"And he still went through with the divorce?" Ian's elevated voice revealed his shock. "I thought..." He hesitated, recovered quickly and when he spoke again he was calm and collected. "How are you taking all this?"

"I'm fine." If it wasn't for the baby, Molly would make a point of getting good and drunk, which would take, at most, one margarita. For all the reassurances she offered, she was mildly surprised to discover it was true. She was going to be all right.

"What are you doing?"

"You mean right this minute?" She returned her father's question with one of her own.

"I don't think it's a good idea for you to be alone at a time like this."

Molly smiled, loving him for his concern. "I've already turned down one invitation for dinner. I prefer my own company. I was thinking of ordering myself a decadent pizza, soaking in a hot bubble bath and being especially self-indulgent for the next few hours."

"I can come over, if you want."

"Dad, I'm a big girl. I'll be fine."

It took her a good five minutes longer to assure him of that. When she hung up the receiver, Molly stood there for a few moments, attempting to connect with her feelings. The afternoon had been spent assuring everyone how well she was taking this divorce business.

Really, what else was there for her to do? Pound the walls and weep with frustration? Wallowing in regrets and recriminations was damn draining. She'd spent the past eight hours on her feet and lacked the energy for a lengthy pity party, especially when it would be so sparsely attended.

In the end, Molly changed into her most comfortable pair of shorts and propped her bare feet against the ottoman. She leaned back and drank a glass of iced tea in front of the television while she listened to the evening news.

The tears that silently crept from the corners of her eyes came unbidden and unwelcome. Rubbing the moisture from her face, she reached for a tissue and blew hard. Her emotions were always close to the surface when she was pregnant, and this was an emotional day.

She certainly wasn't going to beat herself up over a few maverick tears. If she needed to cry over this divorce, then she gave herself permission to do so.

Apparently she needed to cry.

"Oh damn," she said, angry with herself, and reached for the tissue box. It hurt, far more than she'd expected it would. Jordan was free to marry Lesley and live happily ever after with someone else.

Resting her hand on her stomach she closed her eyes. At least she wasn't walking out of this marriage empty-handed. This pregnancy was Jordan's final gift to her.

Determined to ignore her need to weep, she reached for the phone and ordered a deep-dish sausage pizza with extra cheese. Despite everything, she found she was ravenous. Crying demanded a lot of energy and if she needed to fuel those tears, then what better way than with a Chicago pizza?

Her doorbell chimed forty-five minutes later. Carrying a twenty-dollar bill with her, Molly opened the front door to discover Jordan standing on the other side.

His hands were buried deep in his pockets and he looked as if he wanted to be anyplace else but where he was. "You're crying."

She mocked him with a smile. "I never understood why you wanted to be a builder when it's obvious you would have made such a great detective."

He ignored her sarcasm. "Are you going to invite me in or are you going to make me stand on your porch all evening?"

She held open the screen door for him.

He stared at the twenty-dollar bill clenched in her hand. "What's the money for?"

"I thought you were the pizza delivery boy."

Jordan's frown deepened. "Pizza gives you heartburn."

Molly found it ironic that he would remember something like that and not her birthday. "I take it there's a reason you wanted to see me."

He nodded and walked over to the sofa. "What the hell's been going on in here?" he asked when he noticed the discarded tissues. It did look as if she'd held a wake, and in a manner of speaking she had, but it wasn't something she wanted to share with her husband.

Ex-husband, she reminded herself.

"I've got a cold," she lied, grabbing the tissues, wadding them up into one tight ball and holding it with both hands.

"Sit down," he ordered.

"Is there a reason I should?" Jordan looked about as friendly as a porcupine.

"Yeah, I think we should discuss the...pregnancy."

"The word isn't all that difficult," she muttered under her breath, just loud enough for him to hear.

Several uncomfortable moments passed before he spoke. "You're making this damned near impossible."

She was behaving like a shrew, but he'd interrupted her. She was grieving their disillusioned marriage and it was entirely unfair that he should interfere. Especially now, when her pizza was about to be delivered.

No sooner had the thought skipped through her mind when the doorbell chimed. It was the delivery boy.

"Do you mind if I eat while you talk?" she asked. She couldn't see any reason to let the pizza go cold.

Jordan wasn't overly pleased with her request, but he agreed with a hard nod of his head. Molly brought out a plate and dished herself up a piece. She was about to offer him one, when he spoke.

"Do you plan on eating that all by yourself?"

"That was my original intention. You're welcome to some, if you'd like."

Apparently he liked, because he got himself a plate and joined her on the living room floor. They sat, Indian style, knees touching, with the steaming pizza between them.

"You were saying?" she prodded when he didn't immediately resume their discussion.

"I talked to Larry Rife first thing this morning about the pregnancy."

"I bet that surprised good ol' Larry."

"Larry nothing," Jordan snapped. "I wish you'd thought to say something to me."

"Come on, Jordan. You can't tell me the possibility never crossed your mind."

He glared at her. "It never crossed my mind. I assumed you were on the pill."

Molly laughed outright. "Why in the name of heaven would I be taking birth-control pills? I hadn't slept with a man in years."

"All right, you've made your point." He reached for a napkin, wiped his hands clean and set the dish aside. "It was downright stupid of us both, and now we're left to deal with the consequences."

Molly set her own pizza aside, her appetite gone. Her baby wasn't a consequence. Jordan made the pregnancy sound as if it were something unpleasant and best ignored. That irritated her. In fact, it infuriated her.

"Larry's arranging for child-support payments to be sent on a monthly basis."

"I don't want anything from you, especially your money."

"That's too bad, because it's already been arranged."

"Fine." She'd let his money accumulate interest in the bank.

"You'll need to let me know who your physician is, too."

"Why?"

"I changed medical insurance a couple of years back and the physician has to be on their approved list."

All this talk about insurance plans and the like confused her. "I went back to Doug Anderson. I always liked him despite what you say about his golf game. Besides, he spent a lot of time with me after Jeff died."

Jordan flinched at the mention of their son's name, and her heart softened. The wall of tears returned and she reached for a paper napkin and held it against her mouth while she battled for her composure.

Jordan reached out as though to comfort her and stopped himself. Slowly he lowered his arms to his sides. "I'm sorry, Molly, more sorry than I can say."

"Just be quiet," she sobbed. "You aren't supposed to be gentle."

He reached for her then, taking her in his arms and holding her against him, letting his body absorb the sound of her cries. How long he simply held her, she didn't know. She should break away, but she couldn't make herself do it.

"I don't think I've slept two winks since you told me about the pregnancy," he whispered.

"You're right . . . I should have said something right away."

"I can't deal with another baby, Molly. I'm sorry, but I just can't. I'll do what I can to help you through the pregnancy, but I don't ever want to have anything to do with the child."

His words hurt like fire and she jerked herself free of his arms. "Don't worry, you're free now. You've taken care of your responsibilities. I'm sure Lesley's been waiting for this day for a good long while." That was an incredibly bitchy thing to say, she realized, but didn't care.

"What's Lesley got to do with this?"

"You're free," she said, dramatically tossing her arms into the air.

"The hell I am."

"You went before the judge, didn't you?"

It took him far longer than necessary to answer. "As a matter of fact, I didn't."

Chapter Seven

"You mean to tell me we're not divorced?" Molly cried, vaulting to her feet. Here she'd been going through a ritual of grieving. She'd buried her face in a sausage and extra-cheese pizza, and sniffled her way through an entire box of tissues, as she confronted her pain. It had all been for naught.

"We aren't divorced," Jordan said as if he regretted every minute that had passed since he'd made his decision.

"Why aren't we?"

"Because you're pregnant," Jordan returned forcefully.

"So? You just got done saying you didn't want to have anything to do with the baby."

Jordan stuffed his hands in his pockets, and his gaze averted hers. "The pregnancy makes a difference. It's reasonable to wait to refile the papers until after the baby's born. Another few months won't matter one way or another, will it?''

Molly didn't answer him. She sincerely doubted that Lesley would feel that way, but then it wasn't her place to point that out.

An awkward silence fell between them. "How are you feeling?" Jordan asked after what seemed like an inordinately long while. He seemed so ill at ease that it was all she could do not to say something to reassure him.

"I'm fine."

"Morning sickness?"

She shrugged. "A little."

"What about the afternoons?"

So he remembered the afternoon bouts of nausea she'd suffered when she was first pregnant with Jeff. "Some, but not as bad as it was . . . the first time."

He nodded and took his hands out of his pockets.

Molly pushed the hair away from her face. The muggy heat felt stifling. It didn't seem right for them to be sitting in her living room, discussing her pregnancy on the heels of the details of their divorce.

"I don't know how to act around you anymore," she whispered. "You aren't my husband, and yet we're married. I'd made my peace with the divorce and now we aren't divorced. What exactly are we, Jordan?"

The question seemed to cause some internal deliberation. "Couldn't we be friends?"

Molly didn't know how to answer him. Friendship implied camaraderie and rapport, and she wasn't sure they shared that anymore. It implied an ongoing relationship, and being vulnerable to each other.

"Remember how we assured Larry this was going to be a friendly divorce," Jordan prompted.

"That's the problem," Molly said, laughing softly. "The divorce is more friendly than the marriage."

Jordan laughed, too, and it helped ease the tension between them. He sat down on the other end of the sofa.

"A few months won't make any difference," he said, almost as if he were speaking to himself. "Lesley won't mind."

"I'm sure you're right," Molly said, although if she were Lesley she'd have a whole lot more to say on the subject.

"When will you be seeing Doug again?"

"Late Monday afternoon."

"So soon?"

"He wants to closely monitor this pregnancy because I've just come out of Manukua." That and the fact they'd lost Jeff, but that much was implied.

"I see," Jordan commented. "Is his office still downtown?"

Molly nodded.

"That's my project going up, two blocks over. I'll be there Monday afternoon. Why don't you stop by afterward and let me know what the doctor has to say."

"All right," Molly agreed, "I will."

Jordan tried not to think about Molly all morning, but she was like a bad penny, turning up in his thoughts, plaguing him with memories of how good their lives together had once been. All that had changed with Jeff.

He couldn't think about his son and not experience anger. An anger so deep it bordered on rage. Over time Jordan had focused his wrath in just about every direction. At first he blamed the medical profession, Jeff's pediatrician, Molly and finally himself.

If only he'd he gone into Jeff's bedroom that morning. Instead he'd left the house and damned Molly to the agony of finding the body of their lifeless son.

Jordan's fists clenched at his side as the fury worked its way through him. His breathing was hard and heavy and his heart felt like a rock pounding against his ribs. Within a few minutes the anger passed the way it always did, and the tension eased out of his muscles.

Now Molly was pregnant again.

Jordan had delayed the divorce, and even now he wasn't sure why. Molly was right. The baby wasn't going to change anything. Seven, eight months from now it would be born.

It.

He was more comfortable thinking of Molly's pregnancy as an it. Dealing with a tiny human being that cried and laughed and smiled when he recognized his daddy was beyond Jordan's capabilities. He'd keep his distance, Jordan promised himself. He planned never to see this baby, never to hold it, never to love it. But for Molly's sake and perhaps his own, he'd do what he considered best for now.

After Molly's baby was born, Jordan fully intended on having the final papers processed. Then he'd marry Lesley.

He felt better. His life was neatly arranged, tied up in a colorful bow. He was in control again.

He glanced at his watch and exhaled slowly. He was meeting Lesley briefly, returning some blueprints to her office. He wasn't looking forward to this because sure as hell she was going to ask about the divorce.

When he hadn't been plagued with thoughts of Molly, Jordan had been stewing about what he was going to tell Lesley. The truth, of course. But he needed to couch it in a way that assured her of his commitment. Now, however, felt wrong. He'd prefer to give it a few days and sort through his feelings.

If luck was with him, Lesley would be busy and he could hand over the papers to her secretary and make a clean escape. But Luck, the fickle lady she was, hadn't smiled on him in years.

As it happened, Lesley had stepped outside her office and was talking to her secretary when Jordan arrived. He was cursing his fate when she looked up and beamed him a delectable smile.

"Jordan, come and have a cup of coffee with me."

"Sure." For show he looked at his watch, hoping to give the impression he had another appointment and could only manage a few minutes. He followed her into her office, his heart heavy. This could well be the most difficult conversation of his life.

He liked the way Lesley had decorated her office with oak bookcases and a matching drafting table. One thing he could say about Lesley, she had exquisite taste.

"So," she said, automatically pouring him a cup of coffee. "How did everything go in court yesterday afternoon?"

There wasn't any way to say it other than straight out. Perhaps he should reconsider his tactic. He borrowed a trick from Molly instead. "You'd better sit down."

"Sit down?" She raised her eyes from the glass coffeepot until they'd connected with his. "Something's wrong?" she asked and walked around to her side of the desk.

"Not exactly wrong." For all his advice about sitting, he found it necessary to stand himself. "I got a bit of a shock the other night."

"Oh?"

He paused, then decided the only way to say it was straight out. "Molly's pregnant."

"Pregnant?" Lesley made it sound as if she'd never heard the word before. "That must have been a surprise. Who's the father?"

"Ah..." He would have told her then, if she'd given him the chance.

"I imagine it's that doctor friend of hers you mentioned. The one who was with her in Manukua?"

He stiffened and met her gaze straight on. "No. I am."

The mug in Lesley's hand started to shake and coffee splashed over the sides until she managed to set it down on her desk. She sank, slow motion, into her chair.

"I know this is a blow, Lesley, and I can't tell you how sorry I am."

"You and Molly... I see."

Witnessing the pain in her eyes was almost more than Jordan could look at. "I don't have any excuses. It happened while we were in Manukua, while we were held down by the rebel gunfire. We hid in a supply shed and for a time I didn't know if we were going to make it out alive."

"That's your excuse?" she asked, and her voice wobbled with indignation.

"Lesley, I couldn't be more sorry. I wouldn't hurt you for the world."

"Funny, you've done a surprisingly good job of it."
She reached for her coffee in an effort to mask the tears
that brimmed in her pretty dark eyes.

Jordan couldn't remember feeling more of a heel.
Without trying he'd managed to offend the woman he
cared enough about to want to marry.

"You didn't go through with the divorce, did you?"

It surprised him how well Lesley knew him. "No, not
yet. I felt it was better to wait until after the baby was
born."

"I see."

"I don't blame you for being upset," Jordan said,
leaning toward her, his hands clenched together. "I
wouldn't blame you if you threw me out that door and
said you never wanted to see me again, but I hope you
won't. My marriage is dead . . ."

"Apparently not as dead as I once believed," Lesley said, her voice trembling.

"A baby isn't going to solve the problems between
Molly and me. If anything, this pregnancy compli-
cates the issues. We're both having to sort through a lot
of emotional garbage."

"What about the child?" Lesley wanted to know.
"How do you feel about . . . having a child?"

His hands tightened until his fingers ached. "I never
wanted another family. It was understood from the
moment we discussed marriage that there wouldn't be
children. That hasn't changed. Neither Molly nor I had
much say about this new life. She seems to have adjusted to the news without much trouble, but
I . . . frankly, I don't ever plan on seeing the baby. Naturally I'll support the child financially, but I refuse any
emotional involvement."

Lesley's lips quirked upward in a brief smile; at least, Jordan suspected it was a smile. "Jordan, it would be impossible for you not to love this child."

His spine stiffened. Another Jeff. Never. "You can't love what you don't see," he told her confidently.

"You already love this child, otherwise you would have gone through with the divorce," Lesley argued gently. "A pregnancy wouldn't have mattered if you honestly believed you could turn your back on the child."

"It was Molly I couldn't walk away from," he countered. As soon as the words escaped, he realized the profound truth of them, and how deeply they had wounded Lesley. "She had a difficult pregnancy the first time," he added quickly, wanting to undo the damage, already knowing it was too late.

Lesley stood and walked to the window, her back to him. He noticed how rigid she stood, as if she were fighting back the pain. She crossed her arms, her elbows jutting out. "You still love her."

"No," he denied quickly, then added in a thin spiderweb of a voice, "Yes, I suppose I do." He waited, hoping Lesley would turn around, but she didn't. "Don't condemn me for that. Molly was…is my wife. A man doesn't forget his first love."

He saw Lesley's hand move to her face and he realized she was wiping the tears away. It pained him to know he'd hurt her so deeply.

"You might think this an asinine question, but would you be willing to wait for me to divorce Molly?" he asked. "It shouldn't be any longer than a few months. Nothing has to change for us unless you want it to." He'd been as honest with her as he could be, and he hoped she'd take that into consideration.

"I ought to throw you out that door, just the way you suggested."

"But you won't," he coaxed, feeling confident she would have by now, if that had been her intention.

"I... don't know what I should do. Then again, it should be crystal clear," she said with a laugh that sounded more like a sobbing hiccup. "I need time to think this through."

"All right. How long?" They were scheduled to attend a cocktail party with a group of investors over the weekend. Important investors. Even if they didn't arrive together, avoiding each other would be impossible.

"I can't give you an answer to that," Lesley said. "But I will promise to call you once I make up my mind."

Molly stood in line at the hospital cafeteria, deciding between the egg-salad sandwich and the chicken salad, when David Stern cut in front of her.

"Hello again," he said, grinning as he slipped the orange plastic tray next to her own. "I've been waiting to hear from you."

Molly felt mildly guilty for not searching him out, knowing that was what he expected. She liked David, but she didn't want to mislead him into believing they could become involved.

"Care to join me for lunch?" he asked.

"I'd care a whole lot," she joked.

He paid the cashier for her sandwich and milk, plus his own much-larger lunch, and then wove his way between crowded tables to the patio outside.

Molly followed him, grateful he'd chosen to eat outdoors. She loved the sunshine. She set her tray down on the round glass table, under the sheltering shade of the blue-and-yellow umbrella.

"What decadence did you fall into the other night?" David asked.

"A sausage and extra-cheese pizza," she said, opening the wax-sealed milk carton and pouring it into a glass.

"That sounds pretty tame to me. Surely a divorce rated a double Scotch on the rocks."

"I shouldn't drink now," she returned automatically. Her hands froze on the milk carton as she raised her gaze to David's. He might as well know. Her pregnancy wasn't a secret. "I'm pregnant."

David took the information in his stride. "Does your ex know?"

"Yes. It was a shock for us both, but he paid me back in spades."

"How's that?" David asked as he dumped half the pepper shaker on his tuna salad.

"He had his attorney withdraw the divorce petition. I drowned my sorrows in pizza, and cried me a river, only to discover we're still married."

"He wants to reconcile?"

It wasn't polite to laugh, but Molly couldn't help it. "Nothing that drastic. He felt, for whatever reason, that we should wait until after the baby's born. I don't know how his fiancée is going to take this, but that's his problem."

"He's engaged?"

Her life sounded as if it came straight out of a soap opera. "From what I understand, she's perfect for Jordan." Molly raised her sandwich to her mouth. "As you can see I'm not exactly a prime candidate for a relationship. I'd suggest counseling for any man who wanted to become involved with me.''

David laughed. "You sound like you might be needing a friend.''

That was the word Jordan had used, too. Why was it every man in her life suddenly wanted her for a friend? She might as well get used to it. There was only one thing about which Molly was completely certain. She never intended to marry again.

"You're right," she admitted, "I could use a friend.''

"So could I," David said, centering his attention on his lunch. "My wife died the first part of January. We'd been married fifteen years.''

"David, I'm sorry, I didn't know.''

"She'd been sick with cancer for several years. In the end death was a blessing and came as a friend. We both had plenty of time to adjust to the inevitable.''

"Can one ever prepare themselves for the death of a loved one?" Molly questioned, curious. As a nurse, she'd seen death countless times. She'd watched patients struggle and hold on to life until their knuckles were raw from the battle. Yet others gracefully slipped from one life into the next with little more than a token resistance.

"I thought I was prepared," David said quietly, painfully, "but I wasn't. Certainly I didn't want Joyce to suffer any longer. What surprised me was the desperate loneliness I experienced afterward. That lack of connection with one other human being." He stopped eating and reached for his glass of iced tea.

David had walked through the same valley she had, where death cast its desolate shadow. That was what had attracted her to him and why she'd felt an instant kinship with him.

"It's taken me several months to come to terms with Joyce's death. I'm not looking to involve myself in a relationship, if that concerns you. All I want is a little companionship, and it seems to me we're really after the same thing. Just maybe we could help each other."

Molly's eyes met his. "Just maybe we might."

Jordan's pickup was parked outside the house when Molly pulled in behind it and turned off the engine. It might have been better if she'd phoned, but she had agreed to stop off following her appointment with Doug Anderson. Only it was much later than what she'd told him.

It felt strange to ring the doorbell to the home that had once been hers, then stand outside and wait for Jordan to answer. Odd and awkward. She wished now she'd phoned instead. She couldn't be friends with Jordan. Cordial, yes, but their pain-filled history precluded being bosom buddies. She appreciated his concern, but it would probably be best for them if they kept their distance.

When he answered the door Jordan's eyes revealed his surprise at seeing her. The first thing Molly thought was that Lesley was with him and her unannounced arrival would embarrass them all.

"Have I come at an inconvenient time?" she asked, "because I can leave."

"Don't be ridiculous," Jordan answered. He must have recently gotten home himself because he was dressed in his work clothes—khaki pants and a short-sleeved shirt.

"I can quietly leave if...someone's with you."

"I'm alone," he said, drawing her into the house. "What happened? When you didn't show, I contacted Doug's office and got his answering service."

"He was called into the hospital for a delivery. I had to reschedule my appointment. I tried to reach you, but you've got a different cellular number now."

"Damn, that's right. Here, let me give it to you."

"That's all right, " she said, holding up one hand. "It isn't necessary." Carrying his mobile phone number around with her was too intimate, too familiar.

Jordan looked surprised by her refusal. "You might need it sometime."

"I . . . I can always contact your office. They should be able to reach you for me, shouldn't they?"

He shrugged as if it made no difference to him one way or the other, but it did, and she could tell that her refusal had offended him.

"How are you?" he asked, after a short delay.

He wasn't comfortable asking about the baby, she realized, but his question implied his concern. "Healthy as a horse. The morning sickness isn't nearly as severe this time." But she wasn't feeling all that terrific, just then. It was funny how the afternoon bouts of nausea continued to plague her.

He didn't respond, but opened the refrigerator and brought out a pitcher of iced tea. Without asking, he poured her a glass and added a teaspoon of sugar just the way she liked it.

"I thought I'd stop by and explain why I didn't do so earlier," Molly said, positioning herself so that the breakfast counter stood between them. "I . . . won't stay."

"All right, if that's what you want."

Her stomach rolled and pitched and she felt terribly ill all at once. "Would it be all right if I sat down for a minute."

"Of course." Something in her voice must have relayed how ill she was feeling because he took her by the elbow and guided her into the family room.

Sitting helped slightly, and she took in several deep, even breaths. Unfortunately it wasn't enough. She shot up and raced for the bathroom and promptly lost her lunch.

When she finished, Jordan was there with a wet washcloth.

"I'm sorry," she whispered, feeling incredibly weak and close to tears. Once again, her awkward sense of timing had clicked into place.

"You don't need to apologize," Jordan told her, gently guiding her back to the upholstered chair. He brought her a glass of water and she drank thirstily. Jordan stayed by her side, and it seemed he wasn't sure what he should do.

Resting her head against the back of the chair, Molly closed her eyes. "I'll be all right in a minute," she said.

"Relax," Jordan instructed.

Molly felt him place a thin blanket over her. Her mind was drifting into a lazy slumber. She tried to tell herself it wasn't a good idea for her to doze while she was at Jordan's house, but it demanded far more effort than she could muster to pull herself back from the edge of sleep.

Jordan sat across from Molly, watching her while she napped. Dear heaven, she was beautiful. His heart ached as he studied her, hoping she could rest.

The awkwardness between them troubled him. He knew he was to blame and that Molly was protecting herself from any further heartache.

He'd been an ass about the pregnancy. Over the past week he'd made several attempts to reconcile himself to the fact he was going to be a father again. It hadn't worked. His instincts told him to run as fast as he could in the opposite direction.

Molly had his deepest admiration for her bold-faced courage. Dear God, how he wished he could be different. How he wished he could feel the elation he'd experienced when they first learned she was pregnant with Jeff. But that pleasure had been stripped from him the day Jeff had perished.

From the moment Molly told him she was going to have another child, all he'd known was fear. It was like a second skin that clung to his every thought, dictated his actions and taunted him with the feeling nothing in his life would ever be right again.

He longed to give Molly the emotional support she needed and deserved through this pregnancy. But he didn't know if that was possible. This child, innocent and fragile, left him weak with anxiety. Weak in other ways, too, until he damned himself for the coward he was.

A strand of blond hair fell across her pale skin. Jordan yearned to tuck it behind her ear, to hold her head against his chest and wrap her in his arms. He didn't examine his feelings too closely because if he did he might remember how incredible their night together in Manukua had been.

It had been like that in the beginning, after they were first married. Their need for each other had been insatiable, their happiness had brimmed over into every aspect of their lives.

He needed to move away from Molly, Jordan realized, otherwise he'd quickly become trapped in the maze of happy memories.

Cooking dinner seemed the solution, so he moved into the kitchen and brought out a package of steaks. His culinary skill was limited, but he barbecued a decent steak. Salads weren't that difficult, either. He brought the prepackaged lettuce from the refrigerator, a tomato and a green pepper. He chopped the vegetables, feeling especially creative. Every now and again, his gaze involuntarily drifted to Molly.

He must have been glancing her way more frequently than he realized, because the knife sliced across the end of his index finger. A rush of bright red blood followed.

"Damn," he muttered at the unexpected pain. The cut was deep and bled freely. Turning on the faucet, he held his finger beneath the running water and noticed it turn a light shade of pink.

"What happened?" a groggy Molly asked.

"Nothing," he snapped.

"You cut yourself." She was standing next to him. "Let me see."

He jerked his hand away from her. "I told you it's nothing."

"Then let me take a look at it," she insisted. She turned off the water and reached for his wrist, holding it tightly while she wrapped his hand in a clean kitchen towel.

"It's not that bad," Jordan maintained, feeling foolish. It was his own damn fault for being careless.

"You'll live," she agreed. "I'll put a bandage on it and you'll be good as new within a week." She opened the cupboard by the kitchen sink and brought down the bandages, carefully wrapping his index finger in gauze and tape. When she'd finished, she kissed the back of his hand.

The kiss, simple as it was, rippled through him. Unprepared for the impact of her touch, he drew in his breath sharply. Somewhere in the farthest reaches of his mind, the pleasure gripped hold of him and refused to let go. It had been like this in Manukua when she'd placed her arms around his neck and her breath came hot against his throat.

When he dared, he lowered his gaze to Molly's and found that she was staring at him. Her eyes were a reflection of his own, filled with doubt and wonder.

Neither of them moved, neither breathed. It was as though they were trapped in a time warp. He needed to kiss her. Not wanted. *Needed.* He couldn't think about this feeling, couldn't analyze it, knowing that if he did he'd lose courage.

He reached for her and she came into his arms like a soft kitten, purring. She parted her lips to him and trembled as her feminine body adjusted to the hard length of his.

He kissed her again and the pleasure of holding her was his undoing. He trailed his lips down the side of her neck, his tongue dipping into the hollow of her throat.

She might have protested, but he cut her off with the hunger of his kiss, backing her up against the kitchen counter. What had started out gentle and exploratory had quickly altered to a frenzy of need. As his mouth worked against hers, his hands bustled, unfastening the front of her blouse, until he could fill his palms with the weight of her breasts.

"Jordan?" She breathed his name. She had a way of saying it that was unlike anyone else, all breathless and needy. The only time she said it in just that way was when she wanted to make love. It hadn't been so long ago that he'd forgotten.

He moved his hands to her hips and held himself against her, letting her feel the strength of his need. She moaned and met his kiss with a desperation and insistence that was as powerful as his own.

Where he found the strength to break away, Jordan didn't know. "Not in the kitchen," he muttered on a thick guttural sound. He lifted her into his arms and carried her into the family room and placed her on the sofa. His breath was thin and his heart scampered wildly. They were crazy, the pair of them together like this, but he didn't care.

Gently he settled over her, careful to position his weight in such a way not to hurt her or the baby. Her breasts were fuller than he recalled, soft and round. Her nipples pearled up at him and, unable to resist, he locked his lips around one and sucked gently.

Molly buckled against him, and he smiled at the pure glory he experienced, loving her like this. When he lifted his head, he discovered that her eyes carefully studied him, looking for some kind of confirmation, he guessed. With his eyes still on hers, he lowered his mouth to hers.

"I want you," he whispered. His thigh eased hers apart and she let him, welcomed his body as it nestled snugly over her own.

"I know." The words were slow and thick. "I want you, too."

His hands returned to her breasts and she wantonly arched herself against his palms. Her sweet lips were close to his, too close to ignore, and he kissed her, probing his tongue deeply inside her mouth. It swirled over hers in an erotic mating that left them both panting and breathless.

Molly whimpered, sounding very close to tears, and in that moment Jordan died a little. He'd missed her so much, needed her and wanted her and had denied it, hiding his love behind a wall of fear.

Her arms circled his neck and he felt the wetness of her tears. He wanted to tell her how sorry he was, and couldn't, for the lump in his throat. Instead he kissed her gently, lovingly. He kissed her in all the places he'd missed, under her chin, behind her ear and at the edges of her mouth. She clung to him as if he were her source of life.

"I love you," Jordan whispered. "I never stopped, not for a moment."

"What about the baby?"

His world crashed at his feet and shattered in small pieces. "I don't know...I just don't know."

The phone rang then, slicing the moment wide open like a hunting knife ripping through fragile cloth.

"Ignore it," Jordan said.

"No," she insisted, "it might be important."

Nothing was more important than her in his arms, but the phone rang again, sounding urgent. Against his better judgment, he moved away from Molly and reached for the receiver.

"Hello," he barked, irritated at the intrusion.

"Jordan." It was Lesley.

Jordan closed his eyes and groaned.

"Jordan, are you there?"

"Yes." It was all he could do to manage the one word.

"Is something wrong? You don't sound like yourself."

Chapter Eight

"Lesley," Jordan stated, and out of his peripheral vision he caught a glimpse of Molly leaping off the sofa. Quickly she righted her clothes, her movements filled with righteous indignation.

"I thought you'd want to know," Lesley said when he didn't continue.

"Know?"

"What I've decided," Lesley continued.

"Yes, of course." Jordan cupped his hand over the mouthpiece of the receiver. "Molly, wait," he pleaded. They needed to talk, needed to discuss what had happened and make some sense of it.

Molly hesitated.

"Molly's there now?" Lesley asked.

"Yes, listen, could we talk later?"

"That sounds like it'd be for the best. Tomorrow morning?"

"Sure ... sure." All he wanted to do was get off the phone. His main concern was keeping Molly with him, until they'd had a chance to talk this out. It was just like her to run. Just like her to leave him grappling with regrets.

"At ten?"

"Fine. I'll see you then." Jordan replaced the receiver just as Molly walked past him on her way to the front door. "Molly, please wait," he called, nearly stumbling in his rush to reach her before she escaped.

She stopped, her purse clenched against her stomach, for protection, he guessed. Her eyes were leveled at his chest, her breasts heaving slightly in her rush to get away.

"Please don't go. Not until we've had a chance to talk this out."

"No," she answered stiffly. Her eyes, which only moments earlier had been warm with passion, stared back at him empty in an effort to conceal her distress.

"Dammit, Molly, don't do this."

"Me? I'm not the one with both a fiancée and a wife. As far as I'm concerned you've got one too many women. I don't want to see you again, Jordan. I'll have my father notify you when the baby's born and you can have Larry petition the court. All I ask is that you notify me when the divorce is final." Her voice rocked with the strength of her emotion.

"How can you walk away like this after what happened? What nearly happened," he corrected.

"Easy. We've been married and, well, I guess you could say we fall into an old habit. It didn't mean anything, how could it, when you plan on marrying Lesley. We're human, aren't we? It was just one of those things. It happened, and I don't think we should put any credence to it.''

"Habit?" Jordan repeated. "You don't honestly believe that.''

"Come on, Jordan," she said and laughed, but the sound of her amusement was hollow and tinny. "We used to make love on that old couch more often then we ever did on the bed upstairs."

Jordan couldn't disagree with Molly. But kissing her, tasting her, wasn't habit. It had been a rediscovery, a reawakening. He wasn't ready to excuse it away, nor was he willing to leave matters unsettled between them.

"It was far more than habit and you know it," he argued.

Molly sighed with bleak frustration. "I'm not going to stand here and fight with you. If you don't buy my explanation, then make up one of your own. One you're comfortable with." She met his gaze steadily, conviction flashing from her beautiful blue eyes. "What I said stands. I don't want to see you again. Please don't make this any more difficult than what it already is."

"If you're worried about Lesley, then . . ."

"I'm not going to discuss Lesley with you or anyone else."

"It's over between Lesley and me," he said, then realized Molly had walked away. He debated if he should run outside and try one last time to reason with her.

His relationship with Lesley had been a mistake. Jordan didn't know what had taken him so long to realize it. He wasn't entirely sure why he'd ever gotten involved with her. Loneliness, he suspected. He'd been separated from Molly for three long years and his life was empty.

One night, after a couple of drinks, he'd performed a two-bit self-analysis and decided he was over Molly, over Jeff and wanted out of the marriage. He was looking to break new ground in a relationship that wasn't weighted down with grief so heavy it had nearly buried them both.

Jordan felt tired and old and the emotional resilience he'd once prided himself on was long gone. The stark truth was he'd never stopped loving Molly. As hard as he tried, he couldn't make himself not care about her. Oh, he'd managed to convince himself he had for a time, however brief, when he first started dating Lesley. That theory had been blown to hell in a supply hut in Manukua.

The situation might have righted itself naturally if it weren't for the pregnancy. The icy cold fear he experienced each time he thought about this new life they'd created had left him trembling. But then he'd be divorced by now if it weren't for the pregnancy. He didn't know if this new baby was a blessing or a curse.

One thing he did know. He wasn't ready to be a father again.

He didn't know if he'd ever be ready. Or if he wanted to be.

Jordan walked outside, hands in his pockets as he strolled toward Molly. He was willing to swallow his pride in order to keep her with him until they could settle this.

"You're running away again," he said. It was what Molly had done after Jeff had died and now she was guilty of it again, claiming she didn't want to see him anymore.

"I'm running away *again?*" Her eyes filled with fury and were impacted straight at him. "Are you seriously suggesting I was running away when I moved out? Did it ever occur to you, Jordan Larabee, that you all but pushed me."

"That's not true," he answered heatedly, struggling to hold on to his temper.

"You couldn't stand to look at me because every time you did . . ."

"You cried and cried and cried. Dammit, Molly, all you did was mope around the house, sobbing from one room to the next for weeks on end. Jeff was the center of every thought, every conversation. Did you think if you cried long enough and hard enough it would bring him back?"

"I was grieving."

"You didn't have the common decency to tell me you were leaving. I walked in the house and found a stupid note posted on the refrigerator door. You couldn't have told me face-to-face?"

"Why should I? We hadn't talked in weeks. The only reason I left a note," she said, throwing back her head and glaring at him, "was because I feared it'd take a month for you to notice that I'd moved out."

"I handled Jeff's death in my own way," Jordan shouted.

"You handled nothing. You wanted me to pretend he'd never lived . . . you wanted me to continue as if nothing was wrong. I couldn't do it then and I refuse to do it now."

"You're doing it again," he shouted, "throwing Jeff in my face. You're using him as a weapon to beat me up, to tell me how wrong I've been."

"You're the one guilty of repeating the same mistakes," she said, throwing the words at him as if they were steel blades. "You want to pretend this baby isn't alive, either." She flattened her hand over her stomach and her eyes brimmed with tears. "I find it ironic that you accuse me of running away when that's what you've been doing for nearly four years."

Jordan knotted his fists, fighting down the rage. "For once you're right. We have no business seeing each other any longer. By all means, let's not make the same mistakes again."

"That's perfectly fine with me. Go back to sweet, understanding Lesley," Molly suggested, reaching her car. "I'm convinced you're exactly right for each other."

The following morning, Jordan met with Lesley. He wanted to be gentle with her, and sincerely hoped he could break off their unofficial engagement in such a way that left her with her pride intact.

Following his argument with Molly, his nerves were raw. He felt edgy, impatient and so damn weary. He sat up most of the night thinking, not that it had done the least bit of good. In the morning, he felt as if he were walking in a haze. The sensation reminded him of when he'd woken in the hospital after being shot. Drugged, thwarted, restless.

"This time hasn't been easy on either one of us, has it?" Lesley commented, automatically bringing him a cup of coffee. He sat in the leather chair across from her desk and thanked her with a smile. It was going to take a hell of a lot more than caffeine to get him through this ordeal.

"I've done some heavy soul-searching the past couple of days," Lesley said evenly, taking the seat behind her desk. He noticed that she avoided looking directly at him, and guessed she was as uncomfortable as he was.

"What did you come up with?" Jordan asked, sipping his coffee. To his surprise the hot liquid helped clear his head.

"Mostly, I realized that I've been playing a fool's game," she admitted nervously. "You're in love with Molly. I should have realized it when you decided to go after her in Manukua yourself. When you came back, I knew immediately matters between us were different, but I didn't want to own up to it. Then... then at her cousin's wedding, I saw the two of you dancing. It should have been abundantly clear then. You might have said something, Jordan, and spared me this."

She had every right to be angry. Jordan had no defense.

"When I learned Molly was pregnant and you decided to hold up the divorce... well, that speaks for itself, doesn't it?"

"I didn't mean to hurt you." How weak that sounded.

Her hands cradled the coffee mug and she lowered her gaze, taking a moment to compose herself, before she continued.

"I realize now that I was willing to marry you for all the wrong reasons. We'd worked together for several years and were comfortable together, but there's never been any great passion between us. I was willing to marry you, Jordan, because I so badly want to marry. For years I've struggled to build my career and then I woke up one morning and realized how desperately lonely I was. I wanted a loving relationship, needed one."

"We were both lost and lonely souls," Jordan interjected.

"I . . . know I agreed there wouldn't be any children, but I was hoping you'd change your mind later. Talk about living in a fool's paradise."

"I'd like it if we could find a way to remain friends."

Lesley nodded. "Of course. I'm not angry—at least, not at you. You're a good man, Jordan, and I'm hoping you and Molly can work everything out."

"I'm hoping we can do that, too." But it wasn't likely, not now. He stood and set the coffee mug aside. "There's someone out there for you, Lesley. You'll meet him, and when you do you'll know."

October was Molly's favorite month of the year. The winds off Lake Michigan were warm yet, swirling up orange and brown autumn leaves while she walked along the redbrick pathways of the neighborhood park.

At four and half months, her baby was actively making himself known, stretching and exploring his floating world.

Molly hadn't seen Jordan since that last fateful afternoon six weeks earlier. He hadn't made an effort to contact her, and she certainly had no plans to see him. Not after the terrible things they'd said to each other.

In the intervening weeks, Molly was struck by how different she felt. About herself. About life.

At first she assumed it was Chicago that had changed. It had taken her several weeks to realize the Windy City was the same and she was the one who was different.

The years she'd spent in Manukua, she'd been hiding in the shadows of yesterday. Resting in the shade of her loss had become comfortable. It had become home.

Ever since she'd discovered her son dead in his crib, she'd been trapped on a treadmill that continually revolved around the heart-wrenching events of that single Saturday morning. She'd examined those final hours, those final words, those final acts, until the darkness took over and the sum of her life had narrowed down to one single thread of light. She hadn't moved forward since.

Until now.

She'd stepped forward into the sunlight. She'd leaped back into life and experienced joy and laughter once more. Only now could she look with gratitude at the happiness Jeff's short life had given her. The innocence of those few precious months they'd shared would always be with her. The memories of holding him against her breast and feeding him, so pure and perfect. And loving him beyond reason.

God had smiled on her again and she'd been given another child to love. She wanted to laugh when she recalled how shocked and unhappy she'd been when she first realized she was pregnant. She wasn't unhappy now. This baby had filled her life with purpose, had given her a reason to look forward to each new tomorrow.

"I thought you were going to wait for me," David said breathlessly, racing up to her, wearing his blue-and-silver nylon jogging outfit. He slowed his steps to match hers, stopped and braced his hands on his knees while he caught his breath. "How do I look?" he asked, anxiously glancing her way.

"Like an Olympic athlete," she said, lying through her teeth.

David would have laughed if he'd had the energy, Molly guessed. "That's what I like most about you," he said, gasping for breath, "your ability to lie so convincingly."

Molly smiled, squinting into the sunlight.

"How about something to drink," he suggested.

"Sure."

He walked with her to a café across the street from the park and ordered café latte. They sat at one of the outside tables. The umbrella was folded closed and multicolored leaves danced around their feet.

"I've got two tickets for *Les Miserables* for Saturday evening," David mentioned casually, after sipping from the hot drink.

It wasn't the first time he'd hinted that he'd like to take her out. Until now, Molly had declined, but the little-boy expectant look in his eyes caught her attention. She hated to disappoint him.

David had become a good friend in the past six weeks. They'd never officially dated—Molly was uncomfortable with that—but they often walked in the park and occasionally their schedules coincided so they ate lunch together in the hospital cafeteria. But that had been the extent of it.

Molly feared that if she openly dated David, the hospital staff might assume David was her baby's father, and she didn't want to burden him with gossip.

"I'm starting to show just a little," she said, answering his suggestion with a comment.

"Does it bother you to be seen in public with me?"

She laughed softly and shook her head. "No, of course not."

"Then why the hesitation. These are great tickets."

David deserved her honesty. "I'm afraid someone might assume you're the father and I don't want to do anything to taint your reputation."

David laughed outright at that. "I've been waiting for years for someone to taint my pristine reputation. Come on, Molly, let's live dangerously. You'll love the play, and we both deserve a night out, don't you think?"

"We do?"

"I just finished a seven-minute mile, and I told myself when I could do that I was going to treat myself to something special."

"You mean the play?"

"No," he said, reaching for her hand. "A date with you. You'll go with me, won't you?"

Although she wasn't convinced she was doing the right thing, Molly agreed. She was lonesome, and David was her friend.

Jordan wasn't keen on attending this silly play from the first. He'd purchased the tickets six months earlier because Lesley had told him how badly she wanted to see *Les Miserables.*

He'd phoned and reminded her about the tickets, intent on asking her if she wanted the pair herself. It was the first time they'd talked, outside of business, in six weeks. She was the one who suggested they attend the play together, and Jordan figured he owed her that much. Perhaps he'd agreed because he was so damned lonely.

The past six weeks had been difficult. Molly had asked not to see him, and he'd abided by her wishes. That was the end of it, except that he continually toyed with the thought of making one last ditch effort to settle their differences.

He hadn't, for a number of excellent reasons. All right, one excellent reason.

Molly was right.

He'd been running, just the way she claimed. He'd submerged himself in calm, cool waters of denial, refusing to deal with Jeff's death or accept this new life Molly's body was nurturing.

He picked Lesley up at seven and whistled appreciatively when he saw her. She was dressed in a beautiful dark blue full-length silk dress that did wonders for her. The material moved over her hips like a second skin.

"You look fabulous," he said, but even while he was speaking his mind drifted to Molly. She was nearly five months' pregnant by now. Her stomach would be swelling, and the pregnancy would be apparent.

He shook his head in an effort to free himself from thoughts of his wife. He was going to enjoy himself this evening, put his troubles behind him and remember there was a beautiful woman on his arm, who was his friend.

They arrived at the Shubert Theater in plenty of time. Jordan was buying a program when he spotted Molly in the middle of the lobby.

His heart skidded to a sudden halt. She was laughing, her eyes bright with happiness, and Jordan swore he'd never seen anyone, anything, quite so beautiful. She wore a simple white dress with gold sequins along the bodice and hem. The gown wouldn't have looked more elegant on a French model.

Her hair was longer than he remembered. She'd tucked it behind her ears, the length bouncing against the tops of her bare shoulders. Her earrings were a dangly gold pair he'd given her the first Christmas they were married.

Jordan didn't know how long he stared at her. Several moments, he suspected. It took that long for him to notice Molly wasn't alone. A tall sturdy-set man stood at her side. Recognition seized Jordan. Molly was with the same man she'd danced with at Kati's wedding.

She'd had the gall to hurl Lesley in his face while she was involved with someone else herself. Deep, dark emotion bubbled in his soul. It demanded every shred of decorum he possessed not to storm over to her side and cause a scene.

Getting a grip on himself proved difficult, and several minutes passed before he returned to the seat where Lesley was waiting for him.

A few minutes later, Lesley turned, looked at him and whispered, "Jordan, for the love of heaven, what's wrong?"

"Nothing."

"Then why are you so tense?"

"I'm not," he denied sharply. It was apparent he wasn't going to be able to disguise his irritation. "Excuse me a moment," he said as he jerked himself out of his seat.

"Jordan," Lesley said anxiously, "the play's about to start."

Jordan ignored the comment. Thankful he was on the aisle seat he all but raced back to the lobby. Not that he had an iota of an idea what he intended to do once he was there.

The minute he entered the vestibule, Jordan recognized his mistake. Molly was still there with her doctor friend at her side.

She glanced up just then and their gazes collided like giant cymbals. The impact was enough to knock the breath from his lungs. He fully suspected Molly had experienced the same phenomenon. She looked up at her date, gently placed her hand on his forearm and apparently excused herself.

David Stern's eyes sought Jordan out, but he refused to meet the other man's gaze. Instead he centered his concentration on Molly, who was stepping toward him. Her fingers nervously adjusted the strap of her evening bag at her shoulder.

Within seconds they faced each other. Silence followed silence like waves pounding the shore, crashing one after another.

"Hello." It was Molly who spoke first.

"Molly." Burying his hands in his tuxedo pockets became necessary, otherwise he feared he'd drag her into his arms.

Silence again, as he absorbed the sight of her. "How are you feeling?"

"Very well," she told him. She flattened her hand over her stomach and he noticed for the first time the soft swelling there. She was showing. The pregnancy wasn't obvious, but noticeable. "How about you?"

He shrugged. "You look good."

She smiled, lowering her lashes, uncomfortable with his compliment. Only moments earlier he'd wanted to ring her scrawny neck, and one look, one soft whisper, and he was willing to eat out of her hand.

"You seeing much of the good doctor?" His gaze briefly left her to rest on the man waiting impatiently for Molly to return to him. He clenched his back teeth in an effort to resist saying something he shouldn't, although heaven knew he would welcome the opportunity to get face-to-face with the other man.

"Not much. How's Lesley?"

Jordan wondered if she'd seen them together. "She's fine."

The orchestra started to play and once again Molly lowered her lashes. "David and I had better find our seats. It was good to see you again."

His hands remained in his pants pockets and hardened into fists in a desperate effort to contain himself from behaving like a fool. "It was good to see you, too."

"I hope you enjoy the play," she added softly and turned away from him.

He didn't know why Molly continually walked away from him. Every time she did, he felt as if she took a part of his heart with her.

He waited until his wife and Dr. Stern were completely out of his line of vision before he returned to his seat. The play was probably one of the best known and loved of all time, but it couldn't hold Jordan's attention. He doubted that anything could have.

Somehow, through the course of the evening, he managed to say all the right things, comment on the play, even laugh over a joke Lesley made. At intermission he slipped away on the pretense of getting them two glasses of chablis, but in reality he stood alone and waited, hoping for another glimpse, another look, at Molly and her rounding tummy.

He didn't find her again in the crowded lobby. His disappointment was keen when he returned to his seat. The strength of his feelings for her frightened him. The last time they were together they'd come within a heartbeat of making love. He wanted her, needed her, beneath him, making love with him, whispering sweet promises in his ear. He wanted her cuddled against him asleep. He wanted to watch her wake up and smile that dulcet, sexy smile of hers when she found him looking down on her. He wanted her to raise her arms up to him and welcome him into her heart.

How Jordan managed to sit through the remainder of the play, he never knew. A hundred times, possibly more, he toyed with the idea of seeking Molly out and insisting she leave with him, right then and there. Without explanation, without excuse.

He drove Lesley home, battling back a shipload of remorse because he couldn't get away from her fast enough. As always, she was warm and generous and understanding.

Jordan had never thought of himself as an obstinate man, but he had no other accounting for the length of their separation. Now it might be too late. He might have lost her to another man. The thought flashed like quicksilver through his mind, torturing him with the unknown.

There was only one way to find out.

He'd ask.

Two days later, Jordan walked into Ian Houghton's office and shook hands with his father-in-law.

"It's good to see you," Ian said, gesturing toward the high-back leather chair across from his desk. "To what do I owe this unexpected pleasure?"

Ian was always the gentleman, but Jordan knew the old man well enough to recognize the glee in his eyes. Ian had been waiting for this day for a good long while.

Jordan couldn't see any reason not to cut to the chase. "I want Molly back. Is it too late?"

Ian opened his desk drawer and took out a fat Cuban cigar. He offered one to Jordan, who declined. Naturally Ian was going to drag this out as long as he could. He reached for his lighter and the flame curled around the end of the cigar.

"Too late?" he repeated, after taking several puffs of the cigar. "I don't know. You'll have to ask Molly that, not me."

"I saw her Saturday night."

"She was with David?"

Jordan nodded. He almost added how beautiful he'd found her and knew if he did he'd be playing right into Ian's hands. His father-in-law already had the advantage, and Jordan wasn't willing to add to it.

"Has she been seeing a lot of the physician?"

Ian exhaled a puff of thick smoke and the scent of tobacco filled the office. "Not to my knowledge, but my daughter doesn't discuss these things with me."

Jordan was disappointed. He was hoping Ian could tell him more about Molly's relationship with the other man. If he was too late and she was in love with David, he'd be forced to make his peace with that. But if he stood a chance with her again, even a small one, he'd glom on to it and do his damnedest to make their marriage work.

"What about the baby?" Ian asked. "From what Molly said, you don't want to have anything to do with the child."

Jordan didn't respond. Not because he didn't like the question. He didn't have an answer to give the older man. He rubbed his hand down his face and relaxed against the soft leather cushion. "I don't know."

Ian was quiet for a moment before he spoke again. "Did you come here looking for advice?"

"No," Jordan said stiffly, then realized his pride hadn't served him well thus far. "But if you want to offer me some, I'll listen."

Ian arched his thick eyebrows and grinned. "I suggest you make up your mind about the baby before you approach Molly. What you've got here, son, is a package deal. Nothing on this good earth will ever separate my daughter from her child. Not even you, and God knows she loves you."

That tidbit of information should have encouraged Jordan, but it didn't.

He stood, his thoughts as tightly knotted as a tangled gold chain. He desperately wanted Molly. He couldn't bear the thought of loving another child.

He left the office without a word to Ian and stepped outside and walked past his car. He kept on going, block after block, mile after mile. Each step against the pavement moved him forward, but did nothing to solve the dilemma of his heart.

He needed Molly.

But not the child.

Jordan knew the truth of what Ian had told him. Molly and the baby were a package deal. It wasn't one without the other, but the two of them together.

Jeff's chubby happy face, cheerfully smiling at him, returned to haunt Jordan. The pain that sliced through him with the memory was sharper than any physical agony he had experienced. Physical pain he could handle, but not this unending emotional torment.

All at once Jordan was tired. Overwhelmed and lost. He felt as if nothing were real anymore. He continued to walk, but he moved in a haze from one block to the next with no real destination in mind. At least, he didn't realize he'd set his course until he stepped off the curb and crossed the street. Molly's duplex was three doors down.

"Make up your mind about the baby before you approach Molly." Ian's words echoed in the deepest recesses of his heart as he stepped up to her porch.

He didn't have anything to offer Molly, nothing he could say—only that he wanted her, needed her back in his life. Other than that he was as lost now as he had been when he approached Ian.

He had to see her or go insane. Had to know if she still loved him. Had to know if there was one chance in a million that they could mend the rift between them.

He didn't remember ringing the doorbell, but he must have, because the next thing he knew Molly was standing directly in front of him. A thin mesh wire of the screen door was all that separated them.

"Jordan, what are you doing here?" She studied him and he was unable to disguise the murky emotions churning in his mind.

She was shocked to see him and it showed in her eyes. She was dressed in jeans and a loose-fitting shirt. His gaze fell to her waist and he noticed the snap of the jeans was undone to make room for the baby.

The baby.

"Come in," she said, holding open the door for him. His gaze didn't budge from hers.

"Are you alone?" he asked, psychologically distancing himself from her because of the power she wielded. One look, one word, could devastate him.

Molly eyes rounded with surprise. "Yes."

He stepped inside the duplex and closed the door. He studied Molly, wondering what he could possibly say to her that would make a difference.

"Why are you here?" she asked, standing no more than two feet from him.

"Are you in love with him?" Jordan blurted out.

"With David? No, not that it's any of your business."

His heart raced like that of a gazelle's in a dead run. He briefly closed his eyes.

"Why?"

Jordan wasn't a man who trusted words. They had failed him in the past, failed him now when he needed them to explain why he'd shown up on her doorstep, miles from where he'd left his truck. He'd come to her without a single, plausible excuse.

"Jordan," she whispered, her face revealing her confusion.

For hours he'd been numb, walking, thinking, lost in a maze of the impossible. Now Molly was standing within reaching distance and he could feel again. He desperately needed to feel again.

His eyes held hers. "I'm sorry, Molly," he whispered. "So damn sorry." The words barely made it past the knot in his throat. There was more he wanted to say, needed to say, but couldn't.

He watched the tears fill her eyes and her bottom lip start to tremble as she struggled not to give in to the emotion.

Jordan wasn't sure who moved first, him or her. It didn't matter. Within the space of a single heartbeat they were in each other's arms. He felt her tears that coursed unheeded down her face, then wondered if they were his own.

With a deep-seated groan, Jordan kissed her.

The kiss was like fire, a spontaneous combustion. She tasted of honey and passion, and it was impossible to tell which of the two was more potent.

Jordan backed her against the door and she gasped softly when he thrust his tongue deep inside her mouth, stroking and teasing, enticing and mating, until her gasp became a whimper that trembled gently from her lips.

By some fate he found the strength to tear his mouth from hers. His chest was heaving; hers was, too, as he looked down on her. Her hands gripped his shirt and she stared up at him, her mouth parted and moist. Already her lips were slightly swollen from the fierce hunger of his kiss.

"Tell me to leave, Molly. Order me out of here, otherwise I won't be able to keep from touching you. I need you too damn much."

He watched her carefully, knowing the impossibility of what he was asking, praying she wanted him as urgently as he wanted her.

Gradually—he could almost see the wheels of her mind working—a smile formed, starting at the edges of her mouth and working its way to her eyes.

"Are you going to make love to me?" she asked.

He closed his eyes and groaned. "Yes. God, yes."

"What about Lesley?"

He was tugging the shirt over her head with fingers shaking in his need to hurry. "I broke it off six weeks ago."

"You did?"

"Yes." He tossed the shirt aside and freed her breasts. Next his hands were at the zipper of her jeans. She laughed softly and kissed him, using her tongue in ways that caused his knees to buckle.

"What took you so long to come back to me?" she whispered.

Chapter Nine

Jordan lifted Molly into his arms and carried her down the short corridor to her bedroom. He kicked open the door and placed her on the bed. She smiled up at him, her body humming with need. Her jeans were unzipped and she awkwardly slipped them over her hips and down her legs while Jordan undressed with equal haste.

When he was free of the restricting clothes, he joined her on the bed and kissed her. Molly moaned as he rolled onto his back, taking her with him. His tongue plundered her mouth and he buried his hands deep into her hair, holding her prisoner.

It had been so long since he'd touched her like this. Her nerve endings fired to life; the flames of her need raced over her skin until she couldn't bear to hold still. Moving her hips even slightly stroked the swollen heat of his erection until it throbbed and pulsed against her.

Jordan groaned and held her, his fingers like vises against the sides of her face, as his eyes burned into hers. His chest heaved as though it demanded every ounce of strength he possessed not to flip her onto her back right then and there and bury his body in hers.

He seemed to be asking her something, or wanting to, but held back as if afraid.

"Jordan?" His name was a breath of sound and need and love. "Love me," she whispered. "Just love me."

He briefly closed his eyes. "I do." His hands caressed the bare roundness of her hips, then swept down the backs of her thighs. Slowly, careful not to place his full weight on her, he reversed their positions so that he was sprawled across the top of her. His eyes burned into her as he eased her thighs apart and, with a provocative, unhurried ease, positioned himself to enter her.

Molly closed her eyes as the moist tip of his manhood parted the folds of her womanhood. Her breath went shallow as she waited. He held himself stiff and still; much more of this and he'd drive her to the brink of insanity. She arched her hips upward, taking him by surprise. "Jordan . . . don't stop, oh, please."

He moaned and filled her. Molly's groan of pleasure mingled with his as she was enveloped in the hot, moist pleasure of his lovemaking. He gave her a moment to adjust to him and eased still deeper until he was wholly within her.

Only then did he stop. Only then did she resume breathing. Only then did she look up at him, knowing he'd read the love she'd tried so strenuously to hide.

A lone tear rolled from the corner of her eye onto the pillow. Soon her gaze was blurred and Jordan's face was obliterated from her. Bending forward he kissed her. Gently. Sweetly.

Molly curled her legs around his back and laced her arms around his neck and kissed him, her heart bursting with love, until the texture of the kisses changed from tenderness to hunger to raw hunger.

Jordan began to rock against her, his need fierce and primitive, setting a pace so fast and furious that it was akin to being trapped in a rowboat in the middle of a wild winter storm. All Molly could do was cling to him and pray they survived.

With each thrust the tempo increased until Molly was convinced he would propel them both straight off the bed. Not that she would have cared. She panted and whimpered and eventually cried out as her body raced breathlessly toward searing, total completion. When it came, her nails dug into his shoulders as her world shattered into a thousand glorious pieces of light.

Jordan groaned and threw back his head, his eyes tightly closed, and joined her, pumping his body into hers again and again until they were both too weak, too spent, to continue.

Jordan went still and hid his face in the curve of her neck, and the only sound that shattered the silence was that of their breathing.

Jordan woke sometime later, with Molly asleep in his arms. He moved onto his side so he could study her, but he kept her within the wide circle of his arms, unwilling to be separated from her. If he were to die right then, Jordan decided, he would leave this life a happy man.

Never again would he attempt to convince himself he could live without her. That was a fool's game, which he was destined to lose, and he'd learned his lesson well.

He reached out and brushed a strand of hair away from her cheek and noted the track the tears had taken down the side of her face.

Unable to stop himself, he leaned forward and ever so lightly kissed her temple. She stirred and smiled before she reluctantly opened her eyes.

The smile was what did it, that sexy, womanly smile of hers. It created an instant and undeniable hunger within him. He kissed her lips, outlining their shape with his tongue, dipping it erotically into her mouth every now and again.

"Hmm, that feels good," she whispered, wrapping her arms around his neck.

He gathered her close, cradling her in his arms. "You cried," he whispered close to her ear, not understanding her tears. Then again he did. He experienced gratitude, an indebtedness to God for giving him this second chance with Molly. He wasn't going to waste it. Not again.

"I...never thought we'd make love again," she whispered, brushing the hair away from his face. Her gentle hands trembled.

Like Molly, Jordan was caught in the force of a strong, emotional upheaval. His arms circled her waist and they clung to each other.

He could account for every minute of the past three years they'd spent apart. He didn't know what it meant to waste an afternoon, or even an hour. He'd driven himself and his employees hard, tasted the high of success, damning the emotional and physical cost. Anything that would allow him to escape the crippling sense of loss that overwhelmed him every time he thought about Jeff and the breakup of his marriage.

His son was gone, ripped from his arms and his heart, but he still had Molly. And heaven help him, if he lost her, too. He was convinced he'd shrivel up and die. That's exactly what he had been doing in the three years since she'd moved out. Dying. A little more each day, with a pain so profound that it hollowed out his heart.

He wanted this marriage. Needed this time with her. Needed Molly and the healing touch of her love. Their lovemaking had expanded his need. Her touch, her kiss, her generosity, had given him a fresh breath of life. A taste of what their marriage had once been.

Jordan wanted it back. All of it.

He could think of no way to tell her this and so he kissed her. She made a soft, womanly sound that was half whimper, half moan as his hand reached for her breast. His thumb grazed her nipple, which puckered instantly. Smiling at the power he evoked over her body, Jordan fastened his mouth to her breast and sucked gently. He was rewarded with a fractured sound of pleasure as she arched her back off the bed.

Paying equal attention to the other breast produced the same reaction, only now a small cry tumbled from her lips. He felt her shudder of pleasure and continued lavishing attention on her breasts and her mouth.

He'd thought to tease her with the sinfully delicious things he could do to make her want him, but in the end it was Jordan who suffered. Molly looped her leg over his, parting her thighs until his pulsating staff was poised at the opening of her silken heat. He jerked his hips forward, but she moved at precisely the same moment, denying him entrance.

"Molly, for the love of heaven." His hands reached for her waist, dragging her forward. How she managed to maneuver herself on top of him, Jordan was never to know. By some trick, she deftly rolled him onto his back, then gracefully settled her body on top of his, swallowing him whole in one swift, downward movement.

The pleasure was so sharp he nearly passed out with the sheer unexpected nature of it. His hands clenched at her hips to guide and control her movements, but she laughed saucily and gently removed them.

"Hold on, cowboy," she whispered, and her legs tightened against his sides.

Jordan was soon caught up in the wildest ride of his life. She straddled him as though he were a wild bronco, one hand braced against his chest, the other against the headboard as if she were afraid of losing her balance. Her movements were frenzied and wild as she rode him straight into the gates of the keenest pleasure he'd ever known. He buckled against her, arching his back and hips, panting and pleading until she'd milked him dry. Only when she'd given, and taken, everything she wanted did she slow her movements. Panting, she lay down on top of him and buried her moist face against his equally sweat-drenched neck. Simultaneously their chests rose and fell together as the sound of their breathing splintered the silence.

Jordan looped his arms around her and would have released a primal shout of joy, but he hadn't the strength left to do anything more than breathe. And hold this magnificent woman he loved.

Both physically and emotionally drained, they slept again. Jordan woke when the room was pitch-dark, feeling utterly content and satisfied. After three long, loved-starved years, they had a lot of time to make up for, but it didn't need to be done in the space of one night.

Jordan reluctantly eased himself out of Molly's arms, intent on finding himself something to eat. If they were going to continue this kind of physical endurance test, he needed fuel. A peanut butter and jelly sandwich, anything.

"Jordan?" Molly's whisper followed him to the bedroom doorway.

His heart clenched at the dread he heard in her voice, as if she were afraid he was leaving her, sneaking away while she slept. Nothing could be further from his mind.

"I'm hungry."

He heard her soft laugh. "Little wonder." The bed creaked as she climbed off the mattress, reached for something to cover herself with and joined him. Jordan had felt no such compulsion to dress and stalked bare-assed into the kitchen. That room was dim, the moon the only source of light, but when he opened the refrigerator the glow filled the room.

Jordan noticed that Molly had chosen to dress in a long T-shirt that adequately covered her torso and reached the top of her thighs. She looked very much as though she'd spent the past four hours in bed, her eyes hazy with satisfaction, her smile seductive and wanton.

"What are you looking at?" she muttered.

"You."

"I . . . I'm a mess."

"No," he corrected. "I was just trying to decide if I had enough stamina to ravish you again, right here in the kitchen."

Her smile widened, and she blushed prettily. "It wouldn't be the first time you had your way with me in a kitchen."

Jordan's mind grabbed hold of the memory of the early days of their marriage when they'd made love in every room of the house, and he grinned broadly.

"Let's eat. I'm hungry, too."

"There's nothing here," Jordan complained when he examined the refrigerator's contents.

"I've been so tired lately that it's easier to open up a can, or pop something in the microwave."

Jordan knew Molly worked long, grueling hours at the hospital and wanted to ask her to quit, but he hadn't the right. Soon, once they'd settled matters, he'd see to it that she didn't work, not unless she wanted, and then he'd prefer if she did so on a volunteer basis. He was a rich man and there wasn't any reason for her to put in such long hours.

He searched the cupboard next and found a can of peaches in heavy syrup.

"I'll scramble us some eggs," Molly offered.

"Nice idea, but I didn't see any eggs," Jordan said as he ran the peaches under the can opener. The grinding sound filled the silence. He tossed the lid in the garbage, dug into the can with his fingers and produced a slice of peach that he hand-fed to her.

The juice ran down Molly's chin as she ate the fruit. Jordan lapped it up with his tongue, catching the juice just before it dripped onto her shirt. The temptation to kiss her was strong, but he knew the way he was feeling, it wouldn't stop with a kiss.

He fed himself the next slice.

"Jordan," Molly whispered excitedly, her eyes widening. "Feel." She reached for his free hand and pressed it against the small swell of her tummy. "The baby just kicked."

Jordan felt as though she'd thrown ice water in his face. The shock of it rippled over him, and his breath froze in his lungs.

The baby.

Dear sweet God, the baby. For these few idyllic hours he'd managed to effectively push the memory of this second child from his mind.

"Here's your daddy," Molly was chirping softly, unaware of the downward spiral of emotion Jordan was experiencing. He knew he wouldn't be able to hide it much longer. He wanted to jerk his hand away, but she held it flat against her abdomen, her palm pressed against the back of his.

"Molly."

"Did you feel him?" she asked, looking up at him expectantly. The joy drained like fast-flowing water down a sink when her eyes connected with his. She released his hand, but Jordan had the impression she wasn't aware of what she was doing.

Without another word, she turned and marched down the hall.

"Molly," Jordan pleaded, following her, although he didn't know what he would possibly say if she did decide to listen to him.

She gathered up his clothes from the floor, jerking them off the carpet, wadded them in a tight ball and then thrust them into his arms.

"I'd like to talk about this," he said calmly.

"Go ahead." She wrapped her hands around her waist, balanced her weight on one foot and tapped the other in an impatient tempo.

"I'm afraid, Molly."

"Do you think I'm not?"

"It's different for you. The baby's a part of you. Flesh of your flesh...but it's not the same for a man."

"A lot of things are different for a man, aren't they?"

Jordan didn't have an answer to give her. He didn't want to argue with her, didn't want this beautiful time together to end with them hurling ugly words at each other.

"I'm trying, Molly, give me credit for that."

She, too, must have felt the need to preserve what they'd shared. Their peace was fragile and easily destroyed. Molly was as aware of it as he was and seemed equally reluctant to ruin it with another argument.

"Be angry with me in the morning," he suggested. "Hate me then, if you must, but for now let me hold you and love you." He dropped the clothes on the floor and stepped toward her. He was afraid to reach for her, convinced she'd push him away. When he gathered her in his arms, she held herself still. Her arms hung lifelessly at her sides, but gradually he felt the tension ease from her limbs.

"Wait until morning to be angry," he urged softly.

Eventually they returned to the bed and they lay together silently for what seemed like hours. She was cuddled close to his side and they held on to each other as if they heard the high winds of an approaching storm.

"What time is it?" she whispered.

Jordan glanced at the illuminated dial of his watch. "A little after midnight. You'd better get some sleep." One of them should, he mused. For his own part, he didn't want to waste a single minute on sleep.

Molly reached down and covered them with a blanket. It looked for an instant as if she meant to roll away from him, but he reached for her and dragged her back to his side.

"I have tonight," he reminded her. "You can regret it all in the morning if you want, but for the next several hours pretend it doesn't matter, all right?" His hand cupped the fullness of her breast and he experienced a sense of power at the ready way in which her nipple beaded against his palm.

Molly said nothing.

Jordan slipped his hand lower, past the T-shirt to her silky thighs, worming his way between them. She kept her knees tightly clamped together until his finger found her feminine opening and he knew the reason. He grinned. Already she was moist and eager for him.

"I have this theory about regrets," he whispered, working his finger against her pleasure points until her breathing had gone deep and heavy. He all but flipped her onto her back and entered her in one, swift motion. He hesitated until she opened her eyes and glared up at him, openly challenging him.

"If you're going to regret this night," he said with a taunting smile, "let me make it worth your while."

He made love to her slowly, over and over again, until he was convinced they'd both die of pleasure before they lived long enough to rue this one night.

Molly waited for Amanda outside of the secondhand furniture shop early Saturday afternoon. Amanda parked her truck next to Molly's and they both opened their doors and climbed out simultaneously.

When she stepped onto the sidewalk, Amanda's eyes beamed with pleasure. "My goodness, you're showing."

"You can tell?" Molly cupped her hands under her enlarged tummy, making the swelling more pronounced. She looked up at her friend expectantly. "I'm nearly five months now."

"You look wonderful," Amanda said, smiling. "I could be jealous. You're obviously one of those women who positively glow when they're pregnant. Not me. I went through the entire nine months looking like I needed a blood transfusion. If I had any color at all it was a faint tinge of green."

Molly laughed.

"How are you feeling?" Amanda asked.

Molly shrugged. "I've felt better." She hadn't been sleeping well, but she couldn't blame the baby for that. It'd been five days since she'd last seen Jordan, and had yet to decide how she felt about their interlude. She wanted to deny how much she'd enjoyed their lovemaking, but couldn't. He would call her a bald-faced liar and he'd be right. Molly swore that if she hadn't already been pregnant, the night would have produced triplets.

When Jordan did scrounge up the gumption to contact her again, a lot would depend on the mood she was in. Either she'd slam the door in his face, or throw her arms around his neck and drag him back to her bedroom.

He must have intuitively known how ambivalent she felt because he'd completely avoided her. One thing was certain, she wasn't going to seek him out.

"I appreciate you helping me with this," Molly said, leading the way into the shop. She'd purchased the crib a week before, but didn't have any way of getting it to her duplex. Amanda had kindly offered the use of her truck.

"No problem," Amanda returned graciously. "You've helped me more than you'll ever know. It feels good to be able to lend you a hand."

With the help of the shopkeeper, they loaded the crib into the bed of Amanda's truck. Molly led the way to her apartment and together they set it up in the spare bedroom. Since Molly intended on painting the crib, she'd spread newspapers and plastic over the carpet.

"Stay and have some tea with me," Molly offered when they'd finished.

"You're sure you have the time?"

"Of course." She was anxious to get going with the painting, but delaying the project another half hour or so wouldn't hurt.

"I talked to Tommy about us having another baby," Amanda said, while Molly filled up the teakettle and set it on the burner.

"What did he say?" she asked, curious if Amanda's husband felt the same way as Jordan.

"He wants to wait a while first."

"How long?"

"Another six months."

"How do you feel about that?" Molly asked.

Amanda lowered her gaze, then shrugged. "In my heart I know another baby will never take Christi's place, but my arms feel so empty."

Molly understood what her friend was saying. Her arms had felt empty, too. That was why she'd volunteered to work in Manukua. She'd been willing to travel anywhere in the world, endure any hardship, if only it would ease the ache in her soul.

"Do you think that's what concerns Tommy?"

"I don't know. He's afraid we'll lose a second baby too, and I don't think either of us would survive that."

"I... didn't think I'd survive losing Jeff," Molly said, and in some ways she continued the struggle and would for a very long time.

"We agreed that I could go off the pill in three months. It took me six months to get pregnant the first time. The way we figure it, the timing should be about right."

The kettle whistled and Molly removed it from the red-hot burner.

"How's Jordan?" Amanda asked timidly. "Listen, you don't have to talk about your husband if you don't want. It's just that... well, I can't help being curious, especially since he's decided to delay the divorce until after the baby's born."

"He's fine I guess. I... he stopped by last week."

"He did?" Amanda asked excitedly. "Remember when you told me about seeing him at the play? Something about the way you looked when you mentioned him struck me. You're still in love with him, aren't you?"

There wasn't any use in denying it, so she nodded.

"I knew it," Amanda said triumphantly. "What did he want?" She edged closer to the table, then seemed to realize Molly and Jordan's relationship wasn't any of her business. "You don't need to answer that if you don't want."

"Apparently he's broken off his relationship with Lesley," Molly supplied.

"Hot damn!"

"He'd like a reconciliation... I think."

"Double hot damn!"

"But he's still having trouble dealing with my pregnancy."

Amanda's shoulders slumped dramatically as the air rushed from her lungs. "He's afraid. Tommy and I are, too. It's only natural, don't you think?"

"Perhaps, but it's more than fear with Jordan. He's petrified." Molly didn't know what Jordan expected of her anymore. It wasn't as though she could ignore their child. "He's terrified of having any feelings for this child," Molly continued. "I think he's convinced the minute he does that something will happen. He keeps everything bottled up inside. He always has...even with Jeff."

"I feel sorry for him," Amanda said thoughtfully. "He must be miserable, loving you the way he does."

They were both miserable.

Molly poured the tea and the two women chattered for fifteen more minutes. Although they were very different, they'd bonded as friends, both having shared the same heart-wrenching tragedy of losing a child to SIDS.

As soon as Amanda left, Molly changed clothes and got out the paint she'd purchased earlier in the day. She put on an old dress shirt of Jordan's, rolled up the long sleeves and paused to study herself in the mirror.

"Stop kidding yourself," she muttered. Choosing to paint in Jordan's shirt had been a deliberate and willful act. As completely illogical as it was, she felt close to him in this shirt. Years earlier, when they'd been innocent of all that was to befall them, it had been a favorite of hers.

She'd stolen it from his closet when she'd taken her things from the house and moved them into the apartment. For a short time afterward, she feared he'd ask her about it. As the weeks passed, she realized he had so many shirts he wouldn't miss this one.

Wearing it now, while she painted the baby's crib, had been a blatant effort to feel close to him. To bring him closer to her and their baby. In this shirt, she could pretend his arms were around her. In this shirt, she could defy the past.

She was stirring the paint with a flat wooden stick when the doorbell chimed. Feeling thwarted and impatient, she pushed up the sleeves and marched into the living room.

The last person she expected to find on the other side of the door was Jordan. His arms were filled with two heavy brown sacks, and his eyes scooted to hers as if he wasn't sure what to expect.

"I come bearing gifts," he said with a brief, beguiling smile.

"What kinds of gifts?" she asked, crossing her arms, trying to decide what she should do. By all that was right, she should close the door in his face, but she couldn't make herself do it.

"Dinner, with all the fixings," he said. "All your favorites."

Her heart seemed to melt in her breast. "Southern-fried chicken, potatoes and giblet gravy?"

"Or a mild variation thereon."

Molly threw open the screen door. "Come right on in."

Jordan chuckled. "You always could be bought with food."

"If you plan on staying more than five minutes," she warned, "then I suggest you start cooking."

His grin grew broader. Molly followed him into the kitchen and quickly discovered he'd brought far more groceries than necessary for a single meal. He made two additional trips to his car to haul in more groceries.

"I don't mean to be nosy," he said, loading cans into her cupboards, "but where'd you get that shirt?"

Molly's eyes grew round with feigned innocence. "This old thing?"

"It looks amazingly like one of mine."

She fluttered her long lashes. "Are you suggesting I stole it?"

He turned and faced her, hands on his hips. "I am."

She lowered her gaze demurely. "Did you miss it?"

"No, but I've got to tell you, it never looked that good on me."

Molly laughed and, with a turn of her heel, left him and resumed her task in the baby's bedroom. She could hear Jordan working in the kitchen, humming softly to himself as he went about preparing their dinner. Not that it would require any great skill. The deli had already roasted the chicken, which he was attempting to pass off as southern fried, and the mashed potatoes and gravy looked suspiciously as if they'd come from a fast-food restaurant.

No more than fifteen minutes passed before Jordan joined her. He watched her dip the brush in the enamel and spread it evenly over the wood. Molly waited for him to say something, and he didn't for the longest time. She paused in her task and glanced up at him.

"Is it a good idea for you to be painting in your condition?" he asked.

"It's perfectly safe. I asked the man at the hardware store." If he was so concerned, she had an extra brush. She waited, but he didn't volunteer and she didn't ask.

"How was your week?" he asked, and the question was full of implication. It would have been easier to traipse across a mine field than answer it, Molly decided.

Molly reviewed her options. She could lie and tell him everything was just great when she'd been restless and miserable. Or she could admit she hadn't slept a single night through because each time she closed her eyes she remembered how good it had felt to cuddle in his arms.

"I don't know how to answer that, Jordan," she said when she realized it was impossible to be completely honest and keep her pride intact.

"Did you think about me?"

She dipped the brush in the paint and hesitated. "Yes." Turnabout was fair play. "Did you think about me?"

"Every minute of every day. It took me until this afternoon to work up the courage to come back and try again. I never know what to expect from you."

She couldn't deny what he was saying. "Why do we say the things we do?" she asked sadly. "We've both been hurt so badly, and still we do and say such terrible things to each other?"

"I don't know, Molly. All I do know is that I love you."

Under any other circumstances that would have been enough. More than enough. But she wasn't the only one involved. A new life blossomed and grew within her. A new life that couldn't be ignored.

"Say something," Jordan urged, walking toward her.

She hung her head, knowing the instant she mentioned the pregnancy it would erect a concrete wall between them.

Jordan placed his index finger beneath her chin and raised her head until their eyes met. Then, ever so gently, he lowered his mouth to hers. The kiss was long and sweet and potent.

He unfastened the opening to her shirt and cupped her breasts. "Does this bra have to stay on?" he whispered.

"Not particularly."

"Good." He fumbled with the closure at her back that released the front. His hands scooped up the weight of both breasts and he moaned and feasted on each nipple in turn.

Molly didn't know what was keeping her upright. Certainly it wasn't her legs. They felt as if they should have collapsed ten minutes earlier.

Jordan kissed her again and reached for the snap of her jeans. "I didn't stop thinking about us, and how badly I want to make love to you every night for the rest of our lives."

"I . . . I don't know if this is a good idea," she said, garnering the fortitude from somewhere to offer resistance, even if it was only token.

"I know what you're thinking," Jordan countered, his hands and mouth working their magic on her. "You're wondering if all we share is fabulous sex."

Molly's eyes flew open. That wasn't anything close to what she was thinking.

"Maybe we do," he answered, nibbling her ear, using his tongue to probe and flicker over the sensitive skin. "I don't care anymore."

Molly pushed herself free of his arms. "You think all we share is sex?" she repeated, outraged that he would even suggest such a thing. "What about our son, several years of marriage and this pregnancy?" she cried. "Are you saying the only reason you married me was because I was a good lay?"

Molly didn't give him the time to answer. She'd forgotten the paintbrush in her hand, but she remembered it now. Heavy with paint, it dripped onto the back of her hand. Stepping forward, she slapped the paint-soaked bristles across the front of his shirt several times.

"That's what I think of that," she cried.

Chapter Ten

Molly clamped her hand over her mouth, unable to believe she'd actually painted the front of Jordan's shirt. He held up his arms as if he expected to take flight and stared down at his front with a look of horrified surprise.

"Oh, Jordan, I'm sorry," she muttered, setting aside the paintbrush. She reached for a rag, but it soon became apparent that her efforts were doing more harm than good.

"You...painted me."

"You deserved it," she returned, smothering a laugh. As far as she was concerned, Jordan Larabee should be counting his blessings. He was downright lucky that she hadn't taken the brush to his face. To suggest their entire relationship revolved around sex still rankled.

"You might apologize yourself," she suggested while he peeled off the shirt, being careful to avoid spreading the wet paint across his arms and torso.

"All right," he agreed, handing her the damaged shirt, "perhaps I was wrong."

"Perhaps?" She braced her hand against her hip and glared at him, her eyes filled with challenge.

Jordan's Adam's apple bobbed in his throat as he swallowed tightly, holding back a laugh. Apologies had never come easy to him, she realized, and generally he disguised them with humor.

"I was wrong," he muttered, his eyes growing serious, but only momentarily.

She rewarded him with a smile and carried his shirt to the mini washing machine, which was tucked neatly away in a kitchen closet. It was one of those compact washers with the dryer below.

"Don't worry, it's a water-based enamel," she told him, turning the buttons and setting the washer. At the sound of water filling the machine, she turned to him. True, her reaction to his outrageous suggestion had been instinctive, but it was also funny.

Their gazes met and held.

Having her estranged husband walk around her home bare chested offered more of a temptation than Molly was willing to admit. She'd never openly say as much, but Jordan had one fine chest. His shoulders were well muscled and his stomach flat and hard.

"Wait here," she instructed, walking back to her bedroom, removing the old shirt she wore as she progressed. She delivered it to him minutes later, almost hating to part with it. Unfortunately she didn't have anyone to blame but herself.

"Thanks," he mumbled, donning the shirt.

While he was buttoning it up, Molly lowered her gaze. She couldn't look at him and not remember their recent night together. She recalled how she'd felt lying with him, her ear pressed against the wall of his chest. The even, rhythmic beat of his heart had lulled her to sleep, lulled her into believing that there was hope for them, for their wounded marriage.

Molly was well aware of the mistakes she'd made. She deeply regretted them and wanted to right the wrong she'd done to Jordan. If that was possible. Molly was convinced their relationship would always be strained until Jordan properly grieved for Jeff.

They were stuck; traversing down the same dead-end road, and would be until they'd made their peace over the loss of their son. Then and only then would Jordan be free to move forward and accept the baby she was nurturing beneath her heart.

Molly waited until they were sitting across the table from each other, their paper plates piled high with the goodies Jordan had brought with him.

Molly dipped her fork in the steaming heap of mashed potatoes and gravy. "I'd like for us to talk, Jordan. Really talk."

"All right," he agreed, but she heard the hesitancy in his voice.

"I love you so much and this awkwardness between us is hurting us both."

Jordan lowered his fork to the table. His eyes filled with tenderness. "I love you, Molly, so damn much. I can't believe I allowed all this time to pass. I should have gone after you the day you moved out. My foolish pride wouldn't let me."

"I should never have left the way I did. Those days after we buried Jeff were so bleak. I wasn't myself, and I didn't know if I would ever be again.

"I felt like I was walking around in a haze. I was insane with grief and I couldn't make myself snap out of it. You were right when you said all I did was cry."

She hesitated, waited a moment, then continued. "I realize now how terribly depressed I was, but I didn't know it then. I don't think anyone really did."

"I should have helped you."

"You tried," Molly whispered, fighting back tears. "But you couldn't help me. I doubt anyone could have." In retrospect, Molly believed she had probably been close to being institutionalized, and perhaps she should have been.

They each made the pretense of eating, but neither one appeared to have much of an appetite. They didn't speak again, each trapped in the memories of those bleak, pain-saturated months following Jeff's death.

Molly finished her dinner first, dumping her leftovers into the garbage can beneath the sink. "Thank you, Jordan, you're a fabulous cook," she said in an effort to cut through the tension.

"Anytime." He smiled, but his eyes revealed the lack of any real amusement. He stood and carried his plate to the sink, as well.

"Would you like a cup of coffee?" she offered.

"Please."

Her back was to him as she reached for the canister and dumped the grounds into the paper-lined receptacle. The coffee dripped into the glass pot before she broached the subject of their son a second time.

"We need to talk about Jeff."

Her words staggered into the silence.

"Why?"

"I believe it will help us now." She turned around to face Jordan.

He was standing not far from her. Two mugs sat on the kitchen counter where he'd placed them. His hands were clenched at his sides, his knuckles white.

Pretending they were having a normal, everyday conversation, she reached for the mugs and filled them. Jordan joined her at the table. She sat down, propped her elbows against the table and held the mug to her lips. Slowly she leveled her gaze to him, waiting for him to respond.

A full five minutes passed.

"We had the same problem before," he said, sounding perfectly natural. "Jeff is dead—talking about him won't bring him back."

"That's true," she responded evenly. Molly wasn't fooled. Jordan's back was ramrod straight, and it was a credit to the mug maker that the cup withstood the tightness of his grip. She knew the heat from the coffee must be burning his palms, but he seemed unaware of it. "No amount of discussion will resurrect our son," she said, even as the pain sliced open her heart. It still hurt to talk about Jeff, especially with Jordan.

"Then why insist upon dragging that dear boy back into our lives? He's gone, Molly. As painful as that is to accept, he's never coming back."

"Do you think I don't know that?"

"I don't know what you think anymore."

She needed to tread carefully, Molly realized, otherwise they'd fall into the identical trap as before and their discussion would disintegrate into a bitter shouting match. That had been their pattern three years earlier, before they'd blocked each other completely out.

She rested her hand against the soft bulge of her tummy. As she suspected, Jordan's gaze followed the movement of her arm. He quickly looked away.

"I'm pregnant with another child," she said softly.

Jordan kept his eyes trained across the room as if he couldn't bear to be reminded of this second pregnancy. "This child has nothing to do with Jeff."

"That's where you're wrong. This baby has everything to do with Jeff. For nearly four years you've tried to pretend our son didn't exist. You don't want to talk about him. You destroyed every piece of evidence he lived. It isn't as easy as that, Jordan. Jeff was our son and he's indelibly marked our lives, the same way this baby will."

"Listen, Molly, I'm not going to let you force this baby on me," he said, his control snapping. "The pregnancy was a mistake. It should never have happened."

"I refuse to believe that," Molly said as unemotionally as she could, although pain and anger simmered just below the surface. "If it hadn't been for this baby, we'd be divorced by now and you'd be engaged to Lesley. This child is a blessing."

The truth hit her then with as much shock as when she'd walked into Jeff's bedroom that fateful morning. She raised her eyes to Jordan and stared at him as the pain whirled around her like dust in a freak storm. "Maybe I am nothing more to you than a good lay," she choked out.

"No." Jordan's argument was immediate and strong. "That's not true. I love you, Molly. I've never been able to stop loving you."

She so desperately wanted to believe him that she couldn't make herself do otherwise. Her breath was shallow and her lower lip refused to still as she struggled with the effort not to weep. How she managed to hold on to her composure she didn't know. "My baby isn't a mistake, Jordan, not to me."

He didn't respond.

Her hand trembled as she raised it to her face, to brush away a strand of hair that had fallen over her eye. "I'm hoping we can both be mature enough to accept each other's difference of opinion."

"I didn't mean to hurt you," he whispered.

She lowered her head and a tear fell and splashed against the tabletop. "I know."

His hand reached across the table for hers. His fingers locked around hers, his grip tight. "I'd better go."

Just the way he said it made her suspect he wouldn't be back anytime soon. Even knowing that, she couldn't bring herself to suggest he stay.

Jordan was about to walk out of her life and she was about to let him. Another tear fell and bounced against the table, followed by another and then another.

Jordan stood, his gait quick and purpose filled. Abruptly he paused in the doorway leading to the living room, his hands knotted at his sides. He was there for so long that Molly raised her gaze to him. His back was stiff, his shoulders tense.

"Can I come see you again?"

Tightness gripped her throat and when she spoke her voice squeaked as if it badly needed to be oiled. "All right."

He left then and Molly wondered if they were both prolonging the inevitable.

Sometimes loving each other wasn't enough.

Perhaps the kindest thing she could do was cut her losses now and set them both free.

Jordan sat in front of a set of blueprints, drinking a beer. His mind wasn't on his construction company and hadn't been from the moment Molly sashayed her way back into his life. The woman would be the death of him yet.

He hadn't left her apartment more than two hours ago and already he was wondering how long it'd be before he could manufacture an excuse to see her again.

He'd managed to hold off for a week and it'd nearly killed him to stay away that long. He sincerely doubted he'd last another seven-day stretch without being with her, without holding and kissing her again. The woman was an addiction. He could live without lovemaking, but he couldn't live without her. Not again.

Jordan wasn't a man who felt inept around women. He knew he was reasonably good-looking and that women generally found him appealing. He had a nice personality, and the fact he owned a successful business didn't hurt him any.

It wasn't anything he wanted to brag to Molly about, but he could have found plenty of solace after she'd moved out on him, if he'd wanted.

He hadn't.

That was the crux of the problem. He'd never wanted another woman from the moment he'd met Molly Houghton, fresh out of college. He knew the moment they were introduced that this woman with eyes the color of a summer sky would greatly impact his life.

For a time he'd convinced himself that he cared for Lesley, and he had, as a friend. But they'd never been lovers, never shared the deep love and intimacy that had been so much a part of his relationship with Molly. He'd attempted to fool himself into thinking he could put his marriage behind him and make a new life. Lesley had fallen into the scheme herself, eager to marry. She'd admitted as much herself.

Jordan sipped from the beer, wrinkled his nose and set the bottle aside. He didn't like beer, had never liked beer. The only reason he kept it on hand was for his project superintendent, Paul Phelps, who sometimes dropped by the house.

Come to think of it, the last time Jordan had indulged in a beer had been when he and Molly had last lived together and had disagreed over something. He tossed the bottle into the garbage and watched the liquid spill against the plastic lining.

Maybe Molly was right.

She seemed to think all they needed was for him to feel the pain of losing Jeff. Which left him to wonder what he'd been doing for the past four years.

Molly was wrong. He hadn't denied Jeff's existence. He couldn't. He wasn't sure what she wanted, or if he was capable of doing it. Yes, he had disposed of Jeff's personal effects in a timely fashion, but he'd done so in an agony of grief, believing it would be easier for them to deal with their son's death if they weren't constantly being reminded of what they'd lost. In retrospect he could understand why it had been a mistake. They'd both made several blunders in the frantic days following their son's funeral.

For all the unknowns Jordan faced, there were an equal number of facts he did recognize. Molly's pregnancy leaped to mind bright as the noonday sun, blinding him with the glare of truth.

He'd longed to push all thoughts of this baby from his mind and his heart, and to some extent he'd succeeded. But he was well aware that his marriage was doomed beyond hope if his attitude didn't change, and change fast.

He hadn't seen Molly in a week and even in that short time he noticed the subtle changes in her body. It was easy to deny the baby when all evidence of its existence was quietly hidden from view. The baby was making itself more and more evident as time progressed. Within a few weeks Molly would be wearing maternity clothes, and every time he looked at her he'd be reminded of the child.

He rubbed a hand down his face. Despite what Molly claimed, he couldn't force himself into believing this pregnancy was anything but a mistake.

The thought of Molly pregnant deeply depressed him. Needing to escape, Jordan reached for his jacket and left the house. He was in his truck, driving with no destination in mind, before he pulled off the side of the road and parked. There wasn't anyplace he could run. There wasn't anyplace he could hide.

He turned off the engine and, gripping the steering wheel, closed his eyes and desperately sought a solution. He waited several moments for his breathing to relax and his racing heart to return to an even, slow pace.

The temptation to turn his back on the entire situation was strong. He could move his company to another city, and escape his troubles. The Pacific Northwest strongly appealed to him. Within a few years he could establish himself in Seattle, or maybe

Portland. Molly could continue to live here in Chicago and come visit him on weekends. He'd find someone she trusted to leave the baby with. Molly might object, but . . .

The sheer idiocy of the idea struck him all at once and he expelled a giant sigh and restarted the truck. His thoughts as troubled as when he left, Jordan returned to the house.

He sat down in front of the television, and it was a long time before he moved. When he did, it was to turn off the set and go to bed, knowing he'd solved nothing.

"Dad," Molly said as he led her by the hand into her childhood bedroom. "What did you do, buy out the store?" Her mattress was heaped with every conceivable piece of clothing the baby would possibly need, in addition to a car seat, stroller and high chair.

"You said you didn't have anything other than the crib."

"I certainly didn't expect you to go out and buy it."

"Why not? I'm a wealthy old man, and if I can't indulge my grandchild, then what's the use of having all this money."

"Oh, Daddy," she said, throwing her arms around his neck. He, at least, shared her excitement over the baby. It was all becoming so much more real now that she could feel the baby's movements. "Thank you."

"It's my pleasure."

Molly and her father spent the next hour examining each and every item he'd purchased. She held up a newborn-size T-shirt and nearly laughed out loud. "Can you imagine anybody this tiny?"

"That's what I said to the salesclerk."

There were several blankets, all in pastel colors.

"Have you had an ultrasound yet?" her father asked, sounding eager.

"I've had two." Dr. Anderson was being extra cautious with her and this pregnancy, looking to reassure her as much as possible.

"And?" her father prompted.

"If you're waiting for me to reveal the baby's sex, I can't. I told Dr. Anderson I didn't want to know. It doesn't matter to me if the baby's a boy or a girl." She patted her tummy as she realized that in all this time Jordan hadn't once inquired about the baby's sex, although she'd mentioned the ultrasound. He didn't want to know because he wanted nothing to do with their child.

Generally she tried not to think about Jordan in connection with the baby because it resulted in a lengthy bout of unhappiness.

"From that frown you're sporting, I'd say you're thinking about Jordan," her father suggested, breaking into her heavy thoughts.

Molly nodded.

"How are matters between the two of you?"

"I don't know." Rather than raise her parent's hopes for a reconciliation, Molly had decided to play it safe.

"You're seeing him on a regular basis now, aren't you?"

Molly nodded, holding one of the receiving blankets against her front before refolding it and placing it inside the protective covering. "At first he made a point of stopping by once a week and it's more often now."

She wouldn't be all that surprised if Jordan showed up at her apartment after she arrived home. She hoped he would because she was going to need help carrying all the things her father had bought into the house.

"Come downstairs and have a cup of tea with me before you drive home," Ian coaxed.

Molly followed him down the stairs. As she moved down the steps she realized she could barely see her toes. She wasn't a full six months' pregnant and already she was experiencing some of the minor discomforts of the third trimester. Her feet swelled up almost every day now and she'd decided to request a schedule change for part-time employment after Thanksgiving.

"You haven't mentioned your friend Dr. Stern lately," her father said casually. "How's he doing?"

"Just great. We had lunch together last week, and he was telling me about a woman he recently met through a colleague of his. They seemed to hit it off and he's taking her to dinner this week." Molly smiled to herself as she recalled their conversation. David had sounded as excited as a teenage boy about to take his father's car out for the first time. Molly was pleased for him.

David had been a good friend and just exactly what she'd needed those first few weeks. They'd had plenty of in-depth discussions since the day they bumped into each other at her cousin's wedding. He called her occasionally still, but he'd moved on to greener pastures and it was just as well.

"He's a good man," her father commented, carrying the tea-filled china cups to the kitchen table. He chuckled softly. "Jordan came to me, you know."

"No, I didn't."

Her father sprouted a sly smile. "He was afraid it was too late and you and David were already in love."

"When was that?"

Ian cocked his head at an angle as he mulled over his answer. "I can't rightly remember, but it was several weeks back now. It was like someone had hit him over the head with a hard object. Don't misunderstand me, I'm downright fond of Jordan and think of him as a son, but there are times I'd like to slap that boy silly."

"Let me hold him down for you," Molly volunteered, not expecting her father to hear. Apparently he did because he chuckled.

"How's he treating you?"

"With kid gloves." She didn't want to say too much for fear Ian might decide to take matters into his own hands. Jordan had made progress. Not much, but he was trying. She had to believe that or she wouldn't be able to continue seeing him.

"I love him, Dad."

"I know, sweetheart, and he loves you. Somehow I don't think even he realizes how much." Deep in thought, her father sipped his tea. "Be patient with him, Molly."

"I'm trying, Dad. So is Jordan."

"Good."

Ian helped her load the car, and before she left his house Molly phoned Jordan.

"Hello," he answered gruffly on the second ring.

"Hi," she said. It was the first time she'd phoned him, preferring for him to set the course of their relationship. She felt self-conscious now and wished she'd waited to contact him until after she'd arrived home. As it was, her father was standing no more than five feet from her, grinning from ear to ear.

"Molly. I stopped by earlier and you weren't home."

"I'm not home now." So she'd guessed right. Jordan had sought her out. He'd taken her to a movie on

Saturday and brought Chinese takeout with him when he stopped by the house Sunday afternoon. Monday he was going out of town for a brief business trip, and he told her not to expect to hear from him.

"Where are you?"

"My dad's. Listen, he went on a shopping spree and I'm going to need some help unloading my car. Can I bribe you with the offer of dinner?"

"I'll be there in five minutes."

"Jordan, your house is a good ten minutes from mine, in light traffic."

"I know that. I intend to speed. I've missed you, woman. In fact, I think we should give serious consideration to moving back in together, this going back and forth is ridiculous."

Molly's heart cheered at the news, but she didn't agree one way or the other. It was much too soon, but the suggestion was downright tempting.

Jordan was waiting for her in front of her apartment when she arrived. She'd barely had time to put the car into Park when he opened the driver's door and all but lifted her out of the car.

Not giving her time to protest he hauled her into his arms and kissed her as if they'd been apart for months instead of days. The kiss was wet and wild and when he finished Molly was clinging breathlessly to him. She was convinced holding on to him was the only thing that kept her upright.

Jordan buried his face in her neck. "I don't think it's a good idea for you to look at me like that."

"Like what?" she asked in a voice that grew progressively more reedy.

"Like you can hardly wait for me to take you to bed."

Molly blushed profusely, because that was exactly the way she felt. They hadn't made love in weeks, not since the night they'd spent together while she'd wrestled with regrets.

The subject had been on both their minds since that night. Molly couldn't have Jordan touch her and not want him to continue. She was certain he experienced the same physical pull she did. They were young, in love and very human.

The lovemaking had always been good between them, and after their one unforgettable night of passion Molly knew it could easily become dangerously addictive, again.

Jordan knew it, too. Molly was convinced of that. Like her, he was also aware they weren't going to solve their differences on top of a mattress. So they'd both avoided anything but the most innocent of touches. The heated kiss had been a slip on both their parts.

Reluctantly Molly eased herself out of his arms, but it felt cold and lonely outside the circle of his love. "I'll unlock the door," she said, hurrying away from him.

Jordan opened the backdoor of her car and piled his arms full of sacks. "What is all this stuff?" he asked, following her up the brick walkway that led to her half of the duplex.

Molly didn't answer him right away and steered the way into the dark house, turning on the light switches as she went. She paused in the baby's bedroom. She'd decorated it with love and care, anxious for his or her arrival.

"Dad's anxious to be a grandfather again" was the only explanation she gave.

Jordan paused in the nursery doorway, his arms loaded with sacks. For a long moment he didn't step beyond the threshold. Molly turned and waited, her heart pounding like a brass drum, echoing in her ear. After what seemed like an eternity, he came into the room and dropped the packages into the crib, and hurried back out.

Together they must have made five trips or more.

"It looks like he bought out the store," Jordan complained as he brought in the box that contained the high chair. Molly was hoping Jordan would agree to assemble it for her, but she'd broach the subject later.

"Dad's getting excited." So was she, but she found no such enthusiasm in her husband.

Jordan nodded, and decisively closed the door to the nursery. It clicked closed, as though he were shutting all thoughts of their baby off, as well.

Discouraged, Molly went into the kitchen. She didn't want to argue with him, not tonight. She was tired and she'd missed and needed him.

"Do you need help with dinner?" he offered.

Molly shook her head. Hoping inspiration would strike as to what she would cook for dinner, she opened the refrigerator door and gazed inside.

"I meant what I said earlier." Jordan spoke from behind her. His arms came around her and settled lazily over her breasts. "It's crazy for us to live apart when we're husband and wife. I want you in my home and in my bed. I love you, Molly, and you love me."

"I . . . don't think it's a good idea. Not yet."

Somehow he'd managed to unfasten her blouse and his hands roved freely over the fullness of her breasts. Molly closed the refrigerator door and, against every dictate of her will, her eyes drifted closed. Her nipples were so hard they pulsed, but that wasn't the only part of her that was affected by his touch. The lower half of her body felt incredibly heavy and moist.

She rotated her buttocks against his front and with one swirl of her hips felt him grow hard. A lengthy list of seductive promises were hidden beneath a single layer of tight denim.

Jordan turned her around and kissed her, backing her against the refrigerator door.

"I . . . was going to cook dinner."

"Later," he said between heated kisses.

Molly was having trouble keeping a clear head. When she found the strength, she pulled her mouth free from his and panted. "You must be starved by now."

Jordan directed her lips back to his. "You haven't got a clue how hungry I am." He hiked up her skirt until it was gathered like a drawn drape at her waist. Silencing any chance of a protest with a kiss, his hands found their way inside her lace-lined panties.

She knew what he intended to do, and she was intent on letting him, when the baby kicked strong and hard. Jordan must have felt it, too. It would have been impossible for him not to have experienced the sharp, swift motion.

He went still and then expelled his breath in a deep, harsh breath. His head fell forward until he'd braced his forehead against her shoulder.

"Jeff used to do that, too, remember?" It was risky mentioning their son.

Jordan nodded. Easing himself away from her, he righted her clothes and even managed to offer her a shaky smile.

"What was it you were saying about dinner?"

Chapter Eleven

Dipping the crisp dill pickle into the butter-brickle ice cream, Molly swirled it around and carried the coated pickle to her mouth. After she sucked off the ice cream, she repeated the process.

Wearing her robe and shorty pajamas, she stood in the kitchen, depressed and miserable. She hadn't heard from Jordan in three days. Three of the longest days of her life.

He'd helped her unload her car and stayed for dinner, but quickly made an excuse to leave almost immediately afterward. She hadn't seen hide nor hair of him since. Not so much as a phone call.

Something had been troubling him from the moment he'd held her and felt the baby kick. He'd done a good job of trying to hide his distress, but Molly knew. Until that evening, he'd tried to ignore the fact she was pregnant. He couldn't overlook it any longer, however. Not with the evidence so evident!

Molly gently patted her swollen abdomen. The time had come for Jordan to make his decision about her and the baby. Perhaps that was what had kept him away.

The imaginary drumroll had started for them and their marriage. Jordan had to decide what he wanted. It was either love and accept this child or—God, please, no—go through with the divorce. It pained Molly that it seemed to be such a hard decision.

Glancing at the phone, Molly wavered as she toyed with the idea of contacting him herself. She didn't want to lose Jordan, not when they'd worked so hard and covered so much ground. She refused to give up without making one last effort herself.

Swallowing her pride was difficult, but too much was at stake to let a little thing like her ego stand in her way. She'd battled with her pride all too often and regretted it later. If it came down to losing Jordan she didn't want to look back and wish she'd made one simple phone call.

Her hand tightened around the receiver as she dialed his number.

Jordan answered almost immediately as if he were sitting next to the phone, anticipating her call.

"Hello," she said softly.

"Molly." He seemed surprised to hear from her, but the inflection in his voice told her he was pleased.

"I hadn't heard from you in a few days," she said.

"I've been busy."

"I thought that must be it."

He hesitated as if he wanted to say more, then apparently changed his mind.

"How are you?" she asked when there didn't seem anything else to say.

"Good. How about you?"

Molly decided to plunge right in, head first. "The baby and I are doing great."

"I'm glad to hear that."

"I've gotten everything put away in the nursery now. It's organized and ready for when I come home from the hospital." Enough, she wanted to shout. She hadn't meant to stuff the subject down his throat.

"So you've been busy, too."

"Yeah," she said. Closing her eyes, she leaned her shoulder against the wall. "I miss you, Jordan."

He expelled his breath on a lengthy sigh. "I miss you, too."

"Come see me," she whispered, closing her eyes. She needed him with her, yearned for the feel of his arms around her. She longed for him to pick up where he'd left off the last time he was with her.

"You want me to drive over now?" The word contained an element of surprise and reluctance.

"Yes." She decided he needed a bit of incentive. "I'm wearing my baby-doll pajamas." Molly wasn't certain why she found it necessary to tell him that. At one time the black silky top had been Jordan's favorite. It seemed they made love every time she wore them. She'd put them on that evening, wanting to feel close to him, to remember the love they shared.

He hesitated. "Molly, I don't think my coming is such a good idea."

Her eyes flew open with hurt and disappointment. "Why not?"

Once more it seemed to take him a long time to respond. "If I do, we're going to end up making love."

The time to be coy had long passed and Molly smiled softly to herself. "I know."

"You're sure about this?" His voice trembled slightly.

Molly wasn't sure of anything these days. "I'm sure I love you. Is that answer enough?"

Her words seemed to convince him. "I'll be there before you know it."

Molly barely had time to put away the pickles and the ice cream when the doorbell chimed. She hurried to the front door, checked to be sure it was Jordan and then, her hands trembling with eagerness, let him inside.

"Hello," she said, smiling up at him. "You didn't take long."

"No man would with the invitation you just offered."

She laughed and lowered her gaze. "No, I suppose you're right." She was hoping he'd take her in his arms, kiss her until she was senseless and then carry her into the bedroom and make wild, passionate love to her. His reluctance did little for her self-confidence.

"You've got something on your chin," he said, rubbing his thumb over the offending spot. He frowned. "What is that?"

"Ice cream... I was eating it with a pickle and I guess it was messier than I realized." She glanced down at her top and found a couple of spots where the ice cream had dripped.

"How the hell do you eat ice cream with a pickle?" Jordan asked, as if he'd come all this way from his house to hers for a demonstration.

"I'll show you." She walked back into the kitchen, removed both items from the refrigerator and scooped up a dollop of ice cream on the end of the dill pickle. "Generally you need to soften the ice cream in the microwave first, but once you do that it works great. Do you want to give it a try?"

"Why not?" he asked, his eyes smiling.

If she didn't know better, Molly would think he was stalling for time. Her choice of dessert had never overly concerned him before now.

She swirled the pickle around the edge of the ice-cream container and hand-fed it to Jordan. His brows arched upward with surprise. "Hey, it isn't bad. This isn't butter brickle, is it? You hate butter brickle."

"I used to. About a week ago I got this craving for it. I've always heard about pregnant woman getting cravings, but this is the first time it's happened to me."

Jordan lowered his gaze to her protruding stomach. Any increase in her girth since their last meeting would be infinitesimal, but the way he studied her suggested that she'd swollen up like a hot-air balloon.

Feeling self-conscious, Molly tugged the silk robe closed and tied the loop around what had once been her trim waist. Her slender figure was far from svelte these days.

"It wasn't your work that kept you away these past three days, was it, Jordan?" she asked softly.

"No."

At least he was honest enough to level with her.

"I've been doing some thinking," he admitted.

"And?" she prompted when he didn't immediately continue, eager to hear if he'd found any solutions.

"Would you mind if we sat down?" he asked, glancing toward her sofa.

"Of course not." She followed him into the other room and they sat together. Curling her feet beneath her, she leaned against him and smiled softly when he lifted his arm and lovingly placed it around her shoulders.

Molly all but sighed aloud at the warm comfort she felt as he brought her into his arms. She cozied up to him and leaned her head against his chest. It didn't matter if they talked or not, she was content.

He kissed the crown of her head. "I've missed you something fierce."

"Why did you stay away?" The last time they met, he'd asked her to move back into the house with him; now she had to phone and almost plead to see him. What a difference a few days could make.

"I can't think when we're together," he admitted, then added with heavy reluctance, "I needed time to give some thought to us and the baby."

"I assumed as much. Did you come up with any solutions?"

"No."

"I haven't, either." She raised her arms and looped them around his neck. Using her tongue and her mouth, she made lazy circles against his skin, loving the taste and feel of him. She concentrated her attention at the hollow of his throat, gently sucking and kissing his skin. It'd been so long since they last made love and she needed him.

"Molly." Her name was little more than a whispered plea.

"Hmm?" Using the moist tip of her tongue, she worked her way up the underside of his jaw, creating a slick trail that led a meandering path to his lips.

They kissed and it was deep and heady. She sighed as Jordan's hands pushed aside her robe and found her breasts. They'd filled out with the pregnancy and overfilled his palms. Her nipples pearled into tight nubs under his loving attention.

"This isn't going to solve anything," Jordan whispered huskily.

"I'm tired of looking for solutions. I want to make love." She seldom played the role of the aggressor, but when she had in the past, Jordan had enjoyed it as much as she.

Kissing him in the ways she knew he loved, she crawled onto his lap, straddling him with her knees. Freeing his tie, she pulled it loose from the restriction of his button-down collar and tossed it aside. Next she worked free his shirt buttons. The entire procedure had been accomplished with her mouth slanted over his and his hands kneading and molding her breasts.

Jordan stretched out his arm for the lamp and fumbled until he found the switch. Murky shadows blanketed the room and the only sound that could be heard was the mingling of their moans and sighs.

It was while she was on her husband's lap, greedily kissing him and removing his clothes, that their baby decided he intended on becoming a soccer star. The first fluttering of movement they both ignored, but that quickly became impossible as he kicked and prodded against Jordan's tight chest.

Smiling, Molly eased her mouth from Jordan's and sat back. She rested her hands on top of the budding mound of her tummy that was their child. "He's so strong."

Jordan closed his eyes and leaned his head against the back of the sofa.

Molly reached for his hand and pressed it against her stomach. He didn't offer any resistance, which greatly encouraged her. Gradually he opened his eyes and straightened.

"You're going to love him, Jordan," she said softly, wanting to reassure him. "You won't be able to stop yourself."

Again he didn't respond.

"I love you," she whispered, speaking to both the father and the child.

Jordan gently eased her off his lap, stood and paced the room. His steps grew quick, his distress gaining with each stride. "This isn't going to work."

"What isn't?" she asked, her gaze following him as he moved from one end of the room to the other like a confined tiger. Turn, pace, turn, until it was all she could do not to yell at him to stop.

He paused and looked at her in the dim light. "I can't make love to you."

Molly settled back in her seat and wrapped her dignity around her as if she were dressing herself in a mink stole on the coldest night of the winter. "Why not?"

"I don't mean to hurt you, Molly." He repeatedly rubbed the back of his neck, while avoiding looking at her. Much to her irritation, he resumed the incessant walking.

"Tell me," she insisted. Anyone else would have left it at that, saved themselves the humiliation, but she had to know. She demanded to know.

"This embarrasses the hell out of me. It happened the other night, too," he said, as if making a confession. "I can't look at you and not want to make love, but the minute I feel the baby move my desire is gone. It's the same way now. I love you, Molly. God help us both, but right now I'm physically incapable of making love to you."

Molly wasn't sure what she'd expected, but not this. Never this. He was telling her he found her ugly and unattractive. His words hurt as if he'd cut her with a razor blade.

Silence fell as he waited for her to respond.

It took Molly several moments to recover. "Well, that answers that, doesn't it," she said, hoping to hide the extent of her pain. "I don't have a single argument, do I? My figure certainly isn't what it once was."

Climbing off the sofa, she reached for the lamp and turned the knob. Light spilled into the room. Molly would have sold her inheritance not to be wearing these sexy pajamas. She felt like an elephant who'd, by some miracle, managed to stuff itself into a bikini.

Gripping hold of the front of her robe, she walked over to the door and opened it for Jordan. "I'm sorry you have to leave so soon."

"Molly, don't send me away. Not now. Not like this."

She should be awarded a medal for keeping the tears at bay. Holding her chin high and proud, she slowly turned her head so their gazes met. "Please, Jordan, just go."

"The problem's mine, Molly, not yours. You're beautiful. I'm the one who needs help. Let's talk this out."

"Everything's been said a thousand times," she whispered through her pain. "I believe you said it best. This isn't going to work."

Jordan impatiently rammed his fingers through his hair. "I shouldn't have said anything, but sooner or later you were going to suspect something was wrong."

Molly could sympathize with him. He'd backed himself into a corner, but that didn't make any differ-

ence. It would alw...
wasn't going to chang...
world if she continued t...

"You once suggested the...
was the sex ... I was quick ...
minded him, her voice heavy w...
I realize you could be right." Th...
most painful. "Now that I don't ...
speak, there really isn't anything...
there?"

"Molly, that's not true."

"Maybe," she agreed. "Then again maybe not." All
she could be sure of at the moment was that she wanted
Jordan out of her home. If he didn't leave soon, she'd
be in serious danger of an emotional breakdown. Her
pride was already in shreds, and she didn't relish the
thought of humiliating herself further.

"You'll give me a call?" he asked when it became
apparent she wasn't going to change her mind. She
stood like a bouncer holding open the front door,
waiting for him to vacate her apartment.

"I don't know," she whispered, although she seriously doubted that she would. It probably would have
been best to tell him that, but she didn't want to invite
additional arguments.

He paused, his eyes connecting with hers before he
left. In him she read regret and pain and a mixture of
several other emotions. She trained her eyes to stare
straight through him, hoping he'd read her lack of
emotion for blatant indifference.

Of one thing Molly was certain. She'd never be in-
different to Jordan Larabee.

d and Jordan wasn't sure what he ex-
Molly. He'd insulted her, wounded her
just about ruined whatever hope there was of
ing their marriage. Whoever was credited with
ying honesty was the best policy had never been
married, he decided.

He phoned her countless times in an effort to undo
the damage, but Molly had taken to screening her calls
with the answering machine. He'd stopped by her
apartment so often the neighbors had started waving
when they saw him. But he hadn't found the courage
to confront her, especially when she'd made it plain she
wouldn't welcome him after their last meeting.

Damn, but he'd really messed matters up this time.

Nothing short of a blowup with Molly would have
led him to visit his father-in-law. Ian Houghton would
take sheer delight in knowing Jordan had made an ass
of himself for the umpteenth time. But then Jordan
should be accustomed to Ian's belligerent attitude by
now.

His father-in-law was smoking one of his king-size
Cuban cigars, looking downright pleased with himself, when Jordan joined him in his den. Book-lined
walls sat behind him and must have recently been
waxed. The scent of lemon oil permeated the air along
with the fragrant aroma of rich tobacco.

"Jordan, it's good to see you," Ian said as he stood
to greet him. The two men exchanged handshakes.

"You, too." Jordan helped himself to a chair and
rested his ankle against the top of his knee, hoping to
give a carefree, relaxed impression.

"My guess is that you're here to inquire about my
daughter?"

"What makes you think this isn't a social call?" Jordan asked.

Ian laughed. "I know you too well for that. You don't make social calls. If you've taken the time and the trouble to come see me, it has something to do with Molly."

"Don't be so sure. I might be here about money." He'd come to Ian to discuss financing often enough when he was first starting up his construction company. The older man's assistance had been invaluable. He and Molly had spent many an evening with Ian going over the details of a construction project. Molly had never complained and often curled up with a book in this very room while the two men talked business. Jordan missed those times and the closeness the three of them shared.

Jordan met Ian's look. With a knowing smile, his father-in-law puffed at his cigar. "You've got more money than you know what to do with these days. It's not money you're after, it's Molly."

It wouldn't do any good to ease his way into the conversation, Jordan realized. "All right, if you must know, this does have to do with Molly. We had a falling out."

"About what?"

He felt fool enough already without explaining the details. "I insulted her."

Ian relaxed against his leather chair and smiled broadly. "Hell hath no fury like a woman scorned."

"If I wanted to listen to proverbs I'd be reading *Poor Richard's Almanac*. I'm here for advice. I don't want to lose Molly. I love her."

"And the baby?"

Jordan had wondered how long it would take Ian to bring up the pregnancy. "In time I'll grow accustomed to the baby."

Ian's eyes grew dark and serious. The smile Jordan had found irritating seconds earlier folded closed. Ian's eyes sharpened. "My daughter isn't having just any baby, Jordan Larabee, that's your seed she's carrying. It's damn well time you accepted some responsibility."

Jordan stiffened, disliking Ian's tone. "I told Molly from the first that I'd assume complete financial responsibility for the child."

Ian's eyes narrowed as he directed the full force of his outrage on him. "I'm talking about emotional responsibility. Do you think you're the only one who's ever lost a baby? Enough is enough. It isn't any wonder Molly's having medical problems."

Immediate fear stabbed him. "Molly's having problems."

"From what I understand she hasn't been to work all week."

"What's wrong?" Jordan was on his feet by now and unwilling to play a game of cat and mouse while Ian beat him up with the information. He'd ring the old man's neck if Ian didn't tell him and soon.

"You needn't worry, it's nothing serious."

"What's wrong with her?" Jordan demanded, more strenuously this time.

"You'll have to ask my daughter. She gets downright feisty when I do the talking for her," Ian said nonchalantly, then lazily puffed his cigar. Jordan swore the old man did it to hide a smile.

Jordan paced to the other side of the room. "She doesn't answer my calls."

"You might want to visit her."

"Has she been in to see Doug Anderson?" Jordan demanded. The physician was a longtime friend of his, although they hadn't seen each other in several years. Jordan's company had been involved in the construction of the medical building where Anderson practiced.

"I don't know, Jordan. You'll have to ask Molly that yourself."

Jordan glared at his father-in-law and his blatant effort to get him to visit Molly.

"She only tells me a little of what's going on in her life," Ian argued. "My guess is that she has seen the doctor. If she did go, I imagine it's because she's more worried about the baby than herself."

The temptation to drive over to her apartment and find out for himself exactly what was wrong strongly tempted Jordan. He would have if he believed it'd do any good. The minute Molly learned it was him, she simply wouldn't open the door. The woman had a stubborn streak that rivaled his own.

Before he jumped to conclusions, Jordan decided to contact Doug Anderson himself and find out what he could. He left Ian, and sat in his truck and called Doug from his cellular phone.

"Jordan Larabee, my goodness, how long has it been?"

"Too long," Jordan answered, talking inside his truck, parked in front of Ian's house. "I understand Molly's your patient?"

"Yes. I know this bout of flu has been difficult for her, but it's nothing to be worried about. I've given her some medication and suggested she gets lots of rest."

"You're sure it's just the flu?"

"Fairly certain. I've treated several cases in the past couple of weeks with similar symptoms."

"Would you care to get together for a drink?" Jordan asked. "I know it's short notice, but there're a few matters I'd like to talk over with you."

"Sounds like a good idea. Come by the house, why don't you. Mary would love to see you. In fact, she's been wanting to ask you about a contractor. We're looking to have a house built this summer."

Forty minutes later Jordan pulled up in front of Doug and Mary Anderson's three-story brick home.

Mary answered the doorbell and greeted him like a long-lost relative. Jordan regretted having allowed their friendship to lapse. He'd always liked Doug and Mary and couldn't remember the last time he'd talked to them. After Jeff died, and Molly moved out, there hadn't been any room in his life for anything other than work.

Mary insisted on feeding him dinner. Jordan had forgotten how good it was to sit down at a table with friends. The Andersons' three boys were all teenagers. They were tall, good-looking youths, busy with their own lives. Judd at eighteen was the oldest. He was in the kitchen briefly, grabbed a chicken leg off the platter, kissed his mother's cheek and left, claiming he needed to study for an important test with Angela. Peter and Adam had eaten earlier, following football practice, and after shaking hands with Jordan, disappeared.

Jordan found it was almost painful to watch Doug and Mary with their three sons. This was what it would have been like with him and Molly had Jeff lived, he mused. In his mind's eye he could picture his son, wrapping Molly around his little finger, interrupting her scolding with a peck on the cheek and a promise to be home before ten. He could see himself handing his son the car keys so he could study for a test with a girl named Angela.

Following dinner, Doug and Jordan had coffee in front of the fireplace. "I'm worried about Molly," Jordan admitted. "We haven't been on the best of terms lately." He hesitated, then willingly added, "Mostly that's my fault. I've been something of a heel over this pregnancy."

"It's difficult, I know."

Jordan was sure Doug had plenty of experience with couples who'd lost infants to SIDS, but only someone who'd lived through this agony could fully appreciate it.

From what Molly had told him, Doug was closely monitoring this pregnancy. He was pleased his friend had taken special care with her, although he was fairly certain Doug would have done so with any patient who'd previously lost a child.

"I remember how I felt when we learned Mary was pregnant after we lost Joy."

Jordan's head snapped up, certain he'd misunderstood. "Joy?"

"We lost a daughter to SIDS nearly twenty-three years ago. I thought you knew."

Jordan shook his head. Perhaps he did remember Doug and Mary saying something to him at Jeff's funeral, but he'd been in such a state of confusion and pain that it hadn't clicked.

"She was only three months old," Doug added. "It nearly destroyed Mary. Trust me, Jordan, I've walked in your shoes. In some ways I've been in Molly's, too. Because we're both in the medical profession, I know

the torment of doubts she suffered. I felt there must
have been something I should have done, should have
known. After all those years in medical school, and I
couldn't save my own child.''

"How long did it take to get over it?''

Doug sipped from his coffee. "I don't know that I
can answer that, not in months or years at any rate. We
both got on with our lives, but we waited nearly five
years before we decided to have Judd. In many ways it
took me longer to come to terms with Joy's death than
Mary.''

"Molly seems to have dealt with it better than me.''
This was the first time Jordan had openly discussed
Jeff with anyone other than his wife.

"It takes a man longer to process the grief,'' Doug
said. "We aren't as likely to let go of our emotions. I
envied Mary her ability to cry. Men have a far more
difficult time expressing their feelings.''

"How did you feel when you learned Mary was
pregnant with Judd?'' Jordan had scooted forward in
his chair, anxious to learn the answer.

"Scared spitless. I'm not going to tell you it was easy
for either one of us, but it was time to move forward
and we both knew it. Molly's going to do just fine with
this child, and so are you.''

Jordan wished he were as confident as his friend.

"By the way,'' Doug said casually, "I've taken two
ultrasounds of the baby now. Molly's been adamant
about not wanting me to tell her the baby's sex, but if
you're curious I'd be happy to let you know.''

Jordan felt the weight of indecision shift from one
shoulder to the next. He couldn't help wanting to
know, but at the same time he wasn't sure he did. "All
right,'' he found himself agreeing, "tell me.''

"You're going to have a little girl."

A daughter.

For some reason, certainly not one he could explain or understand, Jordan had assumed their baby was a boy. Molly had always referred to her as "him," and he'd believed she'd said so knowingly.

"Congratulations," Doug said, beaming him a wide grin.

"Thanks," Jordan mumbled. His hand was shaking when he set down the coffee mug.

A daughter.

One that resembled Molly with bright blue eyes and pretty blond hair. His heart clenched with such a powerful surge that it was all he could do not to place his hand there and hold on to the incredible sensation. He didn't know that he could name this emotion, but whatever it was, all he could say was that the power of it was tremendous.

"Have you decided on names yet?" Mary asked, joining them.

Jordan looked at his friend's wife as if seeing her for the first time. "No," he whispered.

He stood, and set the coffee aside.

"A daughter," he repeated. He kissed Mary on the cheek, shook hands with Doug as if he were pumping a well for water and let himself out the front door.

So many emotions were coming at Jordan that he didn't know which one to deal with first. He'd just made one of the most profound discoveries of his life.

He wanted this child, wanted her so much it was all he could do not to stand in the bed of his pickup and scream it to the world.

Secondly, he felt like the biggest fool that had ever walked the face of the earth. He'd behaved like a first-rate heel for months. It was a miracle Molly had put up with his stupidity this long. He didn't deserve her, but by heaven, he vowed, he'd find a way of making it up to her.

Jordan resisted the urge to drive directly over to Molly's apartment. He'd give her adequate time to recover from the flu, and then they could sit down and talk this out.

When he walked into the house he saw that the message light on his answering machine was flashing. Praying that Molly had deemed to return his calls, he pushed down the button.

"Jordan, it's Larry Rife. Your office gave me this number. I hope you don't mind me calling you at home, but this is important.

"It's after six now, and I'll be leaving here soon. I got a call from Molly. She asked me to petition the court for a date so the final divorce papers could be filed.

"I thought you'd decided to wait until after the baby was born. I'm confused, but Molly was adamant she wanted to go through with the divorce. Give me a call first thing in the morning if you would. Thanks."

Chapter Twelve

Molly had endured a full week with the worst case of flu in recent memory. The only time she'd been out of the house in five days had been to see Dr. Anderson who offered her sympathy, advice and a mild prescription to see her through the worst of the stomach cramps.

The virus wasn't the only thing keeping Molly down. She'd cried herself a bucket of tears since her last confrontation with Jordan. Her frustration with him that swept through her was far stronger and more debilitating than any virus. Every time she thought about these past few months, she suffered an emotional relapse.

Their marriage was over.

The time had come for Molly to quit kidding herself. For days she'd lain on the sofa and stared into space, reliving the past six months with its tumultuous ups and downs.

She'd almost believed it was possible for them. The bitter disappointment was a difficult pill to swallow when they'd both wanted to salvage their relationship.

Contacting Larry Rife was difficult. She'd barely been able to speak. Her weak voice trembled when she told him the reason for her call. Several times she'd had to stop and compose herself before continuing.

Larry had attempted to persuade her to wait, but she'd insisted. She wanted the divorce over with before she gave birth. That was important to her. Jordan had repeatedly told her he intended to emotionally distance himself from their baby. It would be better, she decided, to completely isolate their child from Jordan with his current attitude. She'd seen no evidence that it would change. The baby deserved better. For that matter so did she.

Having made the phone call, she was left to face the taunts of regrets and doubts. They sat beside her like Job's friends, one on her left, the other on her right, all the while mocking her. She refused to give in to the weakness of tears. She'd shed all she cared to in the past several months.

Now was the time to heal. The time to rejoice in the birth of her son or daughter. The time to pick up the pieces of her life and move steadily forward.

The phone rang and she tensed. Over the past week Jordan had repeatedly called, but she wasn't emotionally or physically up to another confrontation with him. The answering machine had collected his messages. As the messages accumulated, she heard his anger and frustration, followed by his insistence that she have the decency to return his calls. Then he stopped phoning. Abruptly.

The answering machine picked up the call on the fifth ring. Molly tensed until she heard the attorney's voice come over the line.

"Molly, it's Larry Rife. I wasn't able to get hold of Jordan, but I left a message on his machine. I'll get back to you as soon as I've talked to him. I don't suspect that'll take long. If you have any questions, give me a call here at the office. And, Molly—" he paused momentarily "—if you want to change your mind, all you need do is say so. I'll wait for your instructions."

So it wasn't Jordan who was calling. Well, according to Larry, Jordan knew that she intended to go through with the divorce. Or he would shortly. Personally, she didn't want to be around when he heard the news. His temper was infamous.

Molly spent the night on her sofa. The effort it demanded to get up and make her way down the hallway to her bedroom was more than she could muster.

She woke around six and felt wretched, but she wasn't sure if her condition was more physical or emotional. Possibly a combination of both.

She showered, washed her hair and changed clothes. By the time she finished, she was so weak she needed to sit down. Her knees shook and she pushed the wet strands of hair away from her face, pondering just how long it would take to get rid of this bug and resume her everyday life.

The flu, she realized, would gradually work its way through her system, but the deep, brooding sense of loss she experienced over her marriage would require a much longer healing process.

Around eight, Molly managed to eat a piece of dry toast and weak tea. She propped her back against the end of the sofa with a thick pillow and reached for the television controller. It was a sorry day when she resorted to filling her time tuning in to talk shows. Several of her friends were addicted to them, but personally Molly didn't understand what society gained by listening to people who'd claimed they'd talked to aliens and now wanted to marry their pets.

Just when she was comfortable the doorbell chimed, catching her off guard. A glance at the wall clock told her it was barely nine. The buzzer sounded a second time.

The impatient beeps assured it was none other than Jordan. No man on earth rang a doorbell quite like he did. He was always in a hurry and detested having to wait.

"I know you're in there," Jordan shouted from the other side of the door. "Open up."

"Go away," she called back, "I've got the flu."

"I'm not leaving until I've talked to you, so either let me in or call the police right now, because I'll bash in your door if that's what it takes."

The man had no sense. Molly threw aside the comforter and ambled toward the door. Her back ached and she pressed her hand to the small of her spine. She wasn't physically up to a showdown with Jordan, but she had few options. It was face him now or do it later. She preferred to have this scene over with as soon as possible.

She unlocked the door. "It'd serve you right if I did phone the police," she mumbled.

He marched into the duplex like a storm trooper seeking revenge. He was halfway into the living room before he whirled around. His teeth were clenched and the sides of his jaw were white. His eyes were as angry as she'd ever seen them.

"I take it you've talked to Larry."

"Not yet. I decided to have this out with you first."

"I suggest you talk to Larry."

The anger left his eyes as if he were seeing her, really seeing her, for the first time. His fists relaxed and fell slack at his sides.

Molly knew she looked dreadful. It wasn't as if she'd spent the past week at a health spa receiving beauty treatments.

"How are you?" he asked.

Molly closed the front door and leaned against it. "I've never felt better," she lied.

"Sit down," he urged. He moved to help her back onto the sofa, but she pulled away from him, avoiding his touch. She clung to her dignity as if her sanity depended on it, and in many ways it did.

"You wanted to say something," she pressed, willing him to get this over with quickly.

He waited until she'd seated herself and pulled the thick comforter over her legs. For having threatened to bust down her door, now that he had her attention, Jordan didn't seem to know what he wanted to say.

"I had a long talk with Doug Anderson last night."

Of all the things she expected, this came as a surprise. She wasn't sure if he was inviting comment, but she had none to give.

"Mary had me over for dinner," he elaborated. "I saw their three boys."

Molly looked up at him, wondering exactly where this conversation was leading.

He stuffed his hands deep inside his pockets. "I talked to your father, too."

"You certainly made the social rounds."

He smiled briefly at that.

This time the silence was initiated by him. It stretched and stretched, wearing so thin Molly was convinced it would soon break and shatter their taut, courteous discussion.

"Doug and Mary lost a daughter to SIDS over twenty years ago," Jordan said, his voice low and steady. "I wasn't sure if you knew that or not."

"We've talked about it several times." She didn't dare look at Jordan. The minute she did she'd realize how deeply she loved him. It was difficult enough to accept that their marriage was over without being reminded how much the divorce was going to hurt. Jordan had a way about him, a way of turning her will. Even one glance was too risky.

"Larry's message was waiting for me when I got home."

Her gaze was level with his hands. She watched, mesmerized by the expression she read in their movements. First he clenched them, then seemed to force himself to relax. He wiggled his fingers, then clenched them again.

"I can't think of a solitary reason why you should delay the divorce," he surprised her by saying. "I've given you plenty of reasons to wish you'd never met me."

Loving him the way she did, Molly couldn't make herself regret their years together. He'd given her two children, and if for nothing more than Jeff and the life she carried within her now, Molly would always be grateful.

"Jordan, please, I don't have the strength to argue with you. I've made up my mind. Nothing you say now is going to change it."

"I love you."

She closed her eyes. "Love isn't always enough. Please don't make this more difficult than it already is."

"You're sure this is what you want?"

Molly closed her eyes and nodded.

"I don't have the right, but I'm going to ask one small favor of you. Wait." She started to object, but he stopped her. "All I'm asking for is a few months."

"No," she said immediately, "I can't..."

"Until after the baby's born."

For her own peace of mind, Molly didn't know if she could delay it any longer.

"Please," he added almost under his breath.

She'd anticipated his anger, but not this. He seemed almost humble. To the best of her memory, she couldn't remember Jordan asking anything of her. The temptation to give in was strong, like the pull of the tide. It wasn't fair that he solicit this kind of decision now.

The hands that had clenched and unclenched moments earlier flexed and fidgeted before turning palms up as if to silently plead his case.

"On one condition," she said when she found her voice.

"Anything."

"I'll agree to wait, if you don't make any attempt to see me again. It's over as of now, Jordan. I won't make it legal until after the baby's born, because that seems to be important to you, but that's all I'm willing to concede."

"But, Molly..."

"I'm serious, Jordan. Either you agree or I'll go through with the divorce as soon as Larry can arrange a court date. If you attempt to break your word, I'll contact Larry immediately."

What seemed like an eternity passed before Jordan responded. "If that's your one request, then I don't have any choice but to agree."

Molly was feeling wretched, as if she was about to lose her breakfast. "I think it would be a good idea if you left now."

"Can I get you anything?"

"No." She wished he'd hurry. "Please just go."

He turned and walked toward the door, then turned back. "Do you have any names picked out for the baby?"

"Yes." But she didn't understand his sudden curiosity.

"Would you mind telling me?"

"I...I wanted Richard for a boy. I'd like to name him after Dr. Morton. He's back working in Manukua, by the way. He's the kindest, most gentle man I've ever known and he'd be thrilled to pieces to learn I'd named *my* baby after him." She made sure he heard the inflection in her voice.

As far as Molly was concerned, he'd relinquished all rights to their child. The baby was hers and hers alone.

"What about a girl's name?" Jordan pressed.

"Bethany Marie." If Jeff had been a girl they'd planned on the name Lori Jo. They'd sorted through name books for weeks before arriving at a final decision.

Jordan smiled briefly. "That has a nice sound to it. Are you naming her after anyone in particular?"

"Marie's my mother's middle name, and I've always liked the name Bethany."

"I do, too," he said and opened the door.

It seemed to take him a long time to walk away from her. The minute she could, Molly tossed aside the covering and rushed into the bathroom. She didn't know if she'd taken a turn for the worse or if this sudden bout of vomiting was the result of yet another nerve-wracking encounter with Jordan.

A month passed and Jordan didn't hear a word from Molly. Not that he expected he would. But he'd hoped. He'd prayed.

Thanks to Ian and Doug he received regular updates on Molly's condition and savored each report about Bethany Marie's progress. He drilled Doug with so many questions that his friend had eventually handed him a textbook on what to expect the last trimester of pregnancy. Jordan read through it twice.

Thanksgiving was lonely as hell. He flew to Arizona and spent the holiday with his mother, who'd retired there several years earlier. She was pleased and excited to have him. He hadn't been to visit her since Jeff had been born. His life was too crammed full of activity and work to bother with a little thing like maintaining a relationship with his mother. His father had died years earlier while he was in high school, and his sister lived in Oregon.

When he arrived at his mother's home, one of the first things Jordan noticed was a framed photograph of Jeff on top of the television. It disconcerted him so badly that he had to ask her to put it away.

He felt badly about that later, when he returned to Chicago, to an empty house and an emptier life. Molly and tiny Bethany had been constantly on his mind. He wondered how they'd spent the holiday and was tempted to contact Ian and ask.

He rummaged around the house and resisted the urge to phone Ian, knowing he'd made a regular pest of himself recently. He was tired from the weekend travel and the craziness that was involved in flying over a holiday.

He listened to the messages on his telephone answering machine. Nothing important. No one he need call back. No word from Molly.

Walking up the stairs, Jordan passed the room that had once been Jeff's nursery. He hadn't been in the bedroom in more than four years. Not since the day he'd stripped away everything that had been their son's. Not since he'd attempted to wipe out every piece of evidence that Jeff had ever lived.

The fight he'd had with Molly that terrible afternoon would forever stay with him. And her, too, he speculated. He'd carried down the baby furniture and she'd come crying after him, begging him not to give Jeff's things away. She was rooting through the boxes, sobbing hysterically, when the truck driver arrived for the charity pickup.

The man had sat down on the steps with Molly and talked to her in gentle tones. Jordan had stood in the doorway demanding that the agency remove everything. It appalled him now that a stranger had been more sensitive to Molly's pain than he'd been.

Some force he couldn't name directed him to Jeff's room now. He turned the handle and walked inside. The floor was bare. As were the walls. The one item that remained was Molly's rocking chair.

He'd forgotten about that. She used to nurse Jeff by the fireplace in their bedroom. After he died, she'd moved the chair into his room and sat in there alone for hours on end.

Oftentimes he'd come home from work and find her sitting in that very chair, staring into space, tears streaking her face. He guessed she'd spent the entire day there.

Stepping into the bedroom, Jordan sat down in the chair. It creaked as it accepted his weight. He placed his hands over the wide arms and gently rocked back and forth. He closed his eyes and recalled Molly holding Jeff to her breast, talking softly to their son while she gently rocked. Sometimes she sang to him in a beautiful, lyrical voice that vibrated with her love.

It was like a childhood remembrance—something that had happened years and years earlier. A dream from his youth.

Jordan thought again about Doug and Mary Anderson's three sons, and how he pictured Jeff as a young adult, had he lived.

"You're going to have a sister," he whispered.

He pressed his lips together, the sound of his own voice shocking him. It was the loneliness, he decided, that had caused him to talk to a baby who was long dead, long buried, long grieved.

"I have a younger sister," Jordan whispered, then surprised himself by laughing out loud. "She was a pest from the moment she was born. The very bane of my existence until I was a high school senior." He stopped rocking, remembering how fortunate he'd been to have a younger sister who was an "in" for him with the sophomore girls.

Caught up in the memories of his childhood years, Jordan glanced out the window to the manicured grounds of their yard. Perhaps he was overly tired from the trip, he didn't know, but he'd like to have something to blame for what happened next.

In his mind's eye he saw his seven-year-old son racing around, flying a kite. Bethany, who was barely old enough to stand, was reaching toward the sky, laughing with glee. The vision left him as quickly as it came.

He was going insane, Jordan decided. Perhaps he already was.

He didn't know what was happening to him, but all at once his chest felt as if he were being shoved against a concrete wall. His heart thudded like a huge stone. He felt every beat as it pounded and pulsed.

Hot, blistering tears filled his eyes.

A man doesn't cry... A man doesn't cry...

Apparently whoever was supposed to listen, wasn't. Huge sobs racked his shoulders. He hung his head, then covered his face, embarrassed, although no one could see him.

The tears stopped as abruptly and as unexpected as they came, replaced with a savage rage. The force of it threatened to swallow him whole. He'd carried it with him for years, Jordan realized, hauling it around with him like a heavy backpack.

Right or wrong, justified or not, he was furious. Jeff was gone and there was no one to blame. No one he could slam up against a wall and vent his fury upon. No one he could punish and send to jail to rot. And so he'd allowed it to weigh down his life, spitting and spewing with the least provocation.

He vented his anger now, because he hadn't allowed himself to do it back then. Hadn't given himself permission to grieve the way Molly had.

He was a man. A man didn't reveal his pain. A man didn't cry. A man buried his son and then went on with his life. A man held and comforted his wife. A man held his family together. That was what Jordan believed a man should do.

Only he was weeping now.

Weeping alone.

He was angry, and the force of his grief bled like a bad cut across his heart, leaving him yearning for one thing. The end. Deliverance.

For four senseless years, a thick rage had boiled just below the surface of his soul. The cost had been tremendous.

SIDS had taken far more than Jordan's perfect, innocent son. SIDS had robbed him of his wife and his marriage. In many ways, SIDS had claimed a part of his sanity.

Jordan was standing now, his fists clenched at his sides, the chair rocking behind him. He didn't remember coming to his feet. Falling back into the rocker, he closed his eyes and waited for his pulse to return to normal. The room was silent, all but for the heavy thud of his heart, which sounded like a cannon in his ears.

Jordan waited for a release, anything that would end this agony of pain. But he knew that if this catharsis didn't run its course, it would solve nothing. He had walked through the valley, and the only hope he had of reaching the other side was to continue along this same path. His only hope was the promise of the rainbow on the other side.

* * *

"I'm pregnant," Amanda announced when Molly answered the telephone. "I just killed a rabbit."

"Congratulations." Molly didn't have the heart to tell her they didn't test rabbits these days.

"Oh, Molly, I'm so excited I can barely stand it."

She wasn't generally emotional these days, not like she was when she was first pregnant, but she wiped a tear of shared happiness from her eye. "Does Tommy know?"

"Yes. I just called him at work and you know what he did? Oh, Molly, he's so sweet. He started to cry right there on the phone with everyone and his mother watching. Then I started to weep. My goodness, we're a pair. I can't remember when I've been so happy. Yes, I can...but this time, well, this time it's different."

"When are you due?" Molly asked. She was sitting on the sofa, her swollen feet propped up on the coffee table. She'd quit work the week before and had fully intended on putting away her Christmas decorations, but she hadn't found the energy. It would take her a couple of weeks, she speculated, to recoup from the business of the holidays.

"The doctor seemed to think mid-August. I can't believe I'm going to have to spend the hottest part of the summer pregnant. You'd think we'd know how to plan better, wouldn't you?"

Molly wondered if there was ever an easy time to be pregnant. She had another three weeks left before her due date and she felt as big as a house. Ian had become a mother hen, calling her at all times of the day and night. Her father called, but not Jordan. She'd made it plain that she didn't want to hear from him, and apparently he'd accepted the wisdom of her decision.

Fool that she was, Molly couldn't keep herself from hoping he'd call. He'd sent her a Christmas gift by means of her father, and it had depressed her so that she'd wept for days afterward. Ian had wanted to call the doctor. He couldn't understand why a slinky pair of black baby-doll pajamas would upset her so.

She knew that Jordan had company for Christmas. His friend, Zane Halquist, the mercenary he'd hired to get her safely out of Manukua, had flown into Chicago and the two men had spent the holidays together. Molly would have liked to thank Zane herself, had she known he was in town.

Molly had gotten a long letter from Jordan's mother shortly before Christmas and was surprised to learn that he had spent Thanksgiving in Arizona. Martha Larabee told about Jordan asking her to put Jeff's picture away. Her mother-in-law wrote to let her know how badly she felt that she and Jordan hadn't been able to work matters out. She asked Molly to let her know when the baby was born and had mailed a beautiful hand-knit blanket as a Christmas gift.

"I'll save my baby things for you," Molly promised her friend.

"Thanks, but we have plenty of things from Christi."

Molly noted how much easier it was for Amanda to talk about the daughter she'd lost to SIDS now. It was easier for her to discuss Jeff, too. Together they'd found a support group for parents whose children had died and it had helped them both tremendously. Each time she attended a meeting, she thought of Jordan. It was painful, but she came away stronger and more confident.

"I haven't told my dad yet, so I'd better get off the phone," Amanda said.

"Of course. Give him my best."

"I will. And thank you, Molly."

"Me? I didn't do anything."

"You've been the best friend I ever had."

"You've been a good friend to me, too."

"You'll call me when you go into labor," Amanda coaxed.

Everyone seemed to think she was ready to pop. "It won't be for several weeks yet."

"But you'll phone me right away?"

"You're second on my list. My sweetheart of a dad insists on being first."

"Are you going to contact Jordan?"

Molly's gaze fell on the baby blanket his mother had sent. Jordan hadn't been able to bear to look at a framed photograph of Jeff. He wouldn't be able to deal with the labor and birth of this child.

"No," she said sadly. "He doesn't want to know."

"You're sure about that?"

"Positive. Now call your father with the good news and give him my love."

Pleased at her friend's news, Molly hung up the phone and walked into the kitchen. She felt good, but clumsy. As awkward as the broad side of a barn, but good. Although she seemed to require a nap every afternoon, she was full of energy now. After putting away the Christmas decorations, she phoned her father and invited him over for dinner.

Ian arrived promptly at six with a bouquet of flowers and a carton of milk. He patted Molly's tummy and commented on how "full" she looked.

Molly accepted his teasing good-naturedly, kissed him on the cheek and led him into the kitchen.

"How are you feeling?" he insisted on knowing, studying her with an eagle eye.

"I can't remember when I've felt better," she said with a smile, taking the casserole out of the oven and carrying it over to the table.

"I talked to Jordan today," her father commented nonchalantly, smoothing the napkin across his lap.

"Dad, I told you I didn't want to discuss Jordan." Molly had given up counting the ways Ian had of introducing her husband into casual conversation.

"He's worried about you."

"It's an unusually mild winter we're having, isn't it?" she said, setting the serving spoon on the steaming ceramic dish. She waddled over to the refrigerator and brought out the green salad she'd prepared earlier.

"He calls at least once a day to ask about you."

She noticed Jordan didn't inquire about the baby. Molly ignored him and dished up her salad, passing the bowl over to her father. She set the dressing bottle down with a thud. "I was thinking of planting red roses this spring. The same variety Mom loved."

"I was talking about Jordan," Ian returned stubbornly, setting the salad bowl against the table hard enough for it to make a clanging sound.

"I was talking about roses" Molly came back with equal stubbornness.

"He loves you."

"I love that rich deep color of red roses."

Ian slammed his fork down. "I don't know what I'm going to do with the pair of you. Jordan's just as stubborn as you are. Worse. I've told him a dozen or more times that I refuse to answer his questions. If he wants to know how you're doing, he can damn well ask you himself.

"You know what he does, don't you? He phones Doug Anderson right from my own home. When he hangs up, he repeats everything to me as if I needed a physician to tell me about my own daughter."

"Dad," Molly said gently, placing her hand on his. "It's over between me and Jordan."

"Damn fools," he muttered. "The pair of you."

Molly didn't argue. Personally she agreed with him.

It had started out as a perfectly normal January day. Jordan was on the job site talking over a supply problem with Paul Phelps when his beeper went off. Absently he reached for it, removing it from his belt, and glanced at the phone number being printed out across the miniature screen. His heart froze solid when he recognized the caller's number.

"Jordan," Paul's voice broke into his confusion. "What is it?"

"That's Ian. There's only one reason he'd contact me this time of day."

"Molly's having the baby?"

"That would be my guess." Jordan took off in a dead run for the construction trailer. A hundred times, possibly a thousand, he'd warned his crews to put safety first. At the moment, Jordan didn't care what the hell he tripped over as long as he found out what he needed to know.

He punched Ian's home number so hard he nearly jammed his finger. Then he waited. The phone rang a good five times before his father-in-law deemed to answer.

"Jordan, my boy," he greeted jovially, "it didn't take you long to get back to me."

"Where's Molly?" he demanded breathlessly.

"Molly? What makes you think this call has anything to do with my daughter?" He responded to his own sorry joke with a laugh.

"Damn you, Ian, if this is some sort of prank, I don't find it the least bit funny."

Ian's laughter died down. "As it happens, you're right. Molly's on her way to the hospital as we speak. She was adamant that you not know, but I decided otherwise. The problem with my daughter is that I've spoiled her. She seems to think I should do everything she asks."

"Ian, is she all right?"

"I assume so. She sounded fine when she contacted me. A little excited. A little afraid. You are coming, aren't you?"

Now it was Jordan's turn to laugh. "I wouldn't miss this for the world."

Chapter Thirteen

Everything seemed to move in slow motion once Molly arrived at the hospital. The labor room nurse, Barbara, a middle-aged motherly type, was gentle and encouraging as she prepared Molly for the baby's birth.

By the time Molly was situated in bed, connected to the fetal heart monitor, she heard some type of commotion at the nurses' station. It was apparent her father had arrived and wanted to see her.

"That's quite some father you have," Barbara reported when she next came to check Molly. "He's demanding to know what's taking so long. He expected his grandchild to be here before now. He's convinced something has gone terribly wrong."

Ian had been away on a business trip when Jeff had been born and seemed to forget that these matters took their own sweet time.

"You better talk to him," her nurse suggested.

"By all means," she said, "send him in before he makes a genuine pest of himself." Molly couldn't help smiling. She was convinced the last time her father had been anywhere close to a maternity floor had been when she was born twenty-eight years earlier.

At the approach of a contraction, Molly laid her head against the thick feather pillow and breathed in deeply while rubbing the constricting tightness of her swollen tummy. The labor pains were gaining in intensity now, coming every three or four minutes.

Her concentration must have been more centered than she realized, because when she opened her eyes she found Jordan standing at her bedside, his face pale with concern.

Molly stared speechlessly up at him. It had been nearly three months since she'd last seen him, and she damned her fickle heart for the glad way it reacted. It took her a full minute to recover. "How'd you get here?"

"I drove," he answered with a saucy smile. "How are you?"

"Very pregnant." She thought this as good a time as any to remind him of the fact.

"So I see."

Self-conscious, she tugged the thin sheet up to her chin. "How'd you know I was here?"

"Your father phoned me."

Furious, Molly pinched her lips together, suppressing a tirade. Later she'd talk to Ian and let him know, in no uncertain terms, how displeased she was by his treachery. Her father knew she didn't want to see Jordan again. She couldn't have made her feelings any plainer.

"Where's my father?" she asked, looking away from him, simply because it was easier to remember that within a few weeks he would no longer be an important part of her life.

Jordan chuckled softly. "He lit up a cigar and was escorted from the hospital by two orderlies."

"Dad knows better than that."

"He's nervous."

"That's no excuse," she returned primly.

"Perhaps not."

Another pain arrived unexpectedly and Molly closed her eyes at the sudden sharpness she experienced.

"What's wrong?" Jordan asked, instantly sensing her distress. She shut her eyes and shook her head, not wanting to be distracted. Silently she sent loving thoughts to her baby, encouraging him or her through the contraction. Actually she was looking to reassure both the baby and herself. It'd been several years since she'd given birth to Jeff and she didn't recall the labor being quite this intense this soon.

When the pain passed, Molly opened her eyes and discovered Jordan was holding her hand between both of his. His eyes were warm and loving.

The temptation was strong to ask him to remain with her, to help her through this birth the way he had so lovingly stayed by her side when Jeff had been born.

"I don't know that you should be here," she said finally, wishing with all her heart he'd leave now before she broke down and begged him to stay.

"Why not? I was there in the beginning. It only seems fair that I get to see the finished product. Besides there isn't anyplace else in the world I'd rather be," he told her, his voice even and strong. "I love you, Molly, and I love our baby."

Uncertain if she should believe him or not, Molly looked away. She was about to ask him to leave when another contraction struck. Tensing with the pain, she gritted her teeth.

Jordan spoke softly, encouragingly, helping her through the worst of it. When she opened her eyes, she found her husband had helped himself to a chair and had planted himself at her side. His eyes challenged her to send him away. His look told her he wouldn't go without a fight.

"I'm staying," he said, as if he needed to punctuate his determination. "It's my right."

"Why are you demanding parental privileges now? They certainly didn't interest you before."

"I've learned some hard lessons these past few weeks. First and foremost you're right, Molly, I'm going to love our daughter... or son. I won't be able to help myself."

"You're saying that because you know it's what I want to hear." Molly was afraid to believe him, afraid to put her trust in what he was telling her for fear he'd break her heart one more time.

"No, Molly, I've given a lot of thought to this. I already love Bethany... or Richard."

Molly bit into her lower lip. She wasn't in any position to be making sound decisions. Jordan must have sensed her confusion because he brushed the hair from her forehead, bent forward and gently kissed her lips.

"Let me stay with you."

Molly hadn't the strength to refuse. "All right."

As the hours and her labor progressed, Molly was forever grateful Jordan was at her side. He was a tremendous help. He encouraged her and rubbed her backside to soothe away the worst of the pain she ex-

perienced there. He cooled her face with a damp cloth
and gripped her hand when the contractions were at
their worst.

The pains were growing in intensity now. Jordan
verbally charted the seconds for her in a calm, reassuring voice as the hard contractions gripped her body.

"You're smiling," he commented as he wiped the
perspiration from her face with a cold washcloth.
"Care to let me in on the joke?"

"You want a little girl, don't you?"

"What makes you think that?"

"Oh, come on, Jordan, you couldn't be more obvious. You've referred to the baby as Bethany several
times. You haven't called him Richard once."

"Would you mind a daughter?" he asked.

Molly hadn't given the subject much consideration.
She had no preference, she believed, but now she
wasn't so sure. Deep in her heart she might be looking
for a son to replace the one she'd lost. A son to ease the
ache of her loss.

As soon as the thought moved through her head,
Molly realized that wasn't true. No child could ever
replace Jeff. He held his own, distinct spot in her heart.

"All I want is a strong, healthy baby," Molly answered.

"That's what I want, too," Jordan assured her.

Molly rolled her head to one side so she could look
up at him. "Do you want this child?"

"Yes, Molly, I want this baby as much or possibly
even more than I wanted Jeff."

His words confused her and she wasn't sure she
could trust him, especially since her nurse had recently
been in to give her a shot. Barbara had claimed it

would help relax her. "I want to believe you so badly,"
she whispered, "but I don't know if I dare."

"Dare, my love," he whispered, kissing her temple.

When it came time for Molly to be moved from the
labor room into the delivery room, Jordan left her. She
tried to hide how disappointed she was that he'd opted
to stay out of the delivery room, but couldn't.

"Don't look so down in the mouth," Barbara said,
patting her hand. "Your husband will be right back as
soon as he's changed his clothes."

Molly all but wept when Jordan reappeared a few
minutes later, donned in a green surgical top and pants.
She didn't realize there were tears in her eyes until he
lovingly brushed the moisture from her cheekbone.

"It won't be long now," he said, gripping her hand.

Once everyone was in place and situated, Molly
heard Jordan and Doug Anderson chatting. She knew
the two men were acquainted, but she hadn't realized
they were such good friends. Leave it to Jordan to talk
golfing scores with her physician. Both men were so
involved in their conversation they seemed to have
forgotten all about her and the baby.

"Push," Doug urged Molly at the appropriate moment.

"What do you think I'm doing?" she snapped, then
gritted her teeth and strained for all she was worth.

"I don't advise you to cross her just now," Jordan
said to his friend.

"It isn't you who's down here giving birth to a wa-
termelon, buster," she said testily to her husband.

"You're doing great, sweetheart."

This was hard, so much more difficult than what she
remembered.

"Molly, look, you can see the top of her head." Jordan sounded as excited as if he'd won the lottery.

"It could be a boy," she reminded him.

"No way," Jordan said confidently, "that's the hair of a beautiful baby girl. No boy would be caught with soft blond curls."

"You don't know that she's going to be blond."

"Ah, but I do," he said, bending forward and whispering close to her ear. "Just like her mommy."

"It won't be long now," Doug told them both.

"You told me that an hour ago," Molly reminded him waspishly.

"It just seemed like an hour."

Molly glared up at her husband. "Do you want to trade places?"

Jordan's smile was wide and full. "Not on your life. I'm content with my contribution to this effort. In fact, I found it downright pleasing."

"Now isn't the time to joke, Jordan Larabee." No sooner had the words escaped Molly's lips when she felt a tremendous release followed by the husky cry of her newborn baby.

"Welcome to our world, Bethany Marie," Doug Anderson said.

"A girl. We have a girl," Molly whispered. A joy so strong it could barely be contained filled her. Her breathing went shallow and her heart pounded with the force of it. Tears flooded her eyes and ran unrestricted down the sides of her face.

"Come here, Daddy, and meet your little girl, " Doug instructed Jordan.

Molly watched as her husband left her side. Bethany, who didn't appear to be the least bit delighted with her new surroundings, squalled lustily while being weighed and measured. Her tiny face was a bright red as she freely kicked her legs and arms.

The nurse wrapped her in a warm blanket and handed Bethany to Jordan who was sitting down. Molly watched her husband's face as his daughter was positioned in his arms. Jordan looked down on their daughter for several seconds, and then as if he were aware of Molly's scrutiny, looked up.

It was at that moment that Molly saw the tears rolling down Jordan's cheeks.

Jordan crying. It must be an optical illusion, Molly decided. She'd never seen Jordan weep. Not even when they'd buried Jeff.

The tears appeared to embarrass him as the nurse lifted Bethany from his arms and carried her over to Molly. Apparently worn out by the ordeal, Bethany nestled comfortably into Molly's embrace.

"She's perfect," Molly whispered when Jordan came over to stand by her bedside.

"So's her mother." Jordan bent in half and kissed them each on the forehead.

Molly didn't feel perfect. If she were capable of any feeling, it was exhaustion. Time had lost meaning and she hadn't a clue of whether it was afternoon or evening. For all she knew Monday could have leaked into Tuesday. It had been Monday when her water broke, hadn't it?

"You were so confident we were having a girl," Molly said to Jordan.

Her husband raised the back of her hand to his mouth and kissed it. "I have a confession to make."

Now, she mused, was not the time to make any confessions.

"I've known for weeks we were having a daughter."

"How?" she demanded. It wasn't possible.

Jordan's grin rivaled the piercing light of the delivery room. "Doug told me. You claimed you didn't want to know, but I felt no such restraint."

"You did know." She yawned loudly, barely able to stay awake.

"I love you, Molly, more right this moment than I believed it was possible to love anyone."

"I love you, too."

He brushed the hair from her face. "Go ahead and sleep—you're exhausted. We'll have plenty of time to talk later."

Molly was eager to comply. She sighed, completely and utterly content.

Molly might be exhausted, but Jordan had never been more wide-eyed and excited in his life. Ian was pacing the waiting room floor when Jordan arrived through the swinging doors, still in his surgical greens.

"Well, for the love of heaven, don't keep me in suspense any longer," Ian said impatiently. "I haven't been this nervous since Molly's mother went into labor."

"Mother and child are doing fine." It was payback time. For once Jordan had the information Ian wanted, but it wasn't in him to keep the older man guessing. Not when it was all Jordan could do not to shout out the wonderful news.

"Boy child or girl child?" Ian barked.

"You have a beautiful granddaughter."

"A little girl." Ian slumped down into a chair as if his legs had suddenly turned to rubber. "By heaven, a girl." He reached for his cigar in his shirt pocket and stuck it in his mouth. It looked as though Ian had taken to chomping on it to ease the tension and had chewed it down to a nub.

"Molly's fine?" he asked, looking up at Jordan.

"Sleeping. You can see her for a moment, if you want."

Recovering quickly, Ian stood and rubbed his hand down his face. "I don't know about you, young man, but I can't remember a more wretched night."

Jordan disagreed. This had to be one of the most fantastic nights of his life.

"I'm headed home, and the minute I arrive I'm pouring myself a stiff drink of Scotch." He looped his arm companionably over Jordan's shoulders. "Would you care to join me?"

Jordan was sorely tempted. "Give me a rain check. I think I'll stick around here for a little while longer. I want to watch Bethany receive her first bath. The nurse said she'd let me hold her again once they're finished."

Ian slapped his back affectionately. "What about you and Molly? Are you going to be all right?"

"I think so."

"Good." Having said as much, Ian left the hospital.

Jordan spent the next hour with his newborn daughter, then slipped into Molly's room. As he suspected, his wife was sound asleep. He intended on only staying long enough to be sure she was resting comfortably. There'd be time enough in the morning for them to talk. But he soon discovered he couldn't make himself walk away from her.

He felt extraordinarily happy. Tired, too, but unlike any other kind of exhaustion he'd ever experienced. Sitting beside her, he studied the face of the woman he loved. His heart was so full, it felt as if it would burst wide open.

He must have fallen asleep because the next thing he knew Molly's hand was on his head.

"Jordan," she whispered, sounding dreamy and vague, "what are you doing here?"

He'd rested his eyes for a few moments, he recalled, crossed his arms against the side of the bed and leaned forward, but he hadn't intended to rest more than five minutes.

"It seems to me," he said, yawning loudly, "this was where the conversation got started sometime yesterday afternoon. You asked me what I was doing here then, too."

Her smile was the most beautiful sight he'd ever seen, with the one exception of her holding Bethany while they were in the delivery room.

"How are you feeling?" he asked.

She didn't answer him. "You wept."

The display of tears embarrassed him, but he didn't regret them. They'd come of their own accord without him realizing what was happening. His emotions had taken control more than once in the past few weeks.

"I don't ever remember seeing you cry," she continued.

The strong male image had been too important for that. "I've done my fair share of weeping lately," he confessed, "sitting in Jeff's nursery and dealing with some deeply buried emotions."

Molly looked as if she were about to break into tears herself. They should be celebrating instead of crying, but he refused to chastise her for tears. Not when he'd done it so often in the past.

"I'm sorry, Molly, for being such a heel. Can you find it in your heart to forgive me?"

"Yes," she said, bypassing the tightness in her throat. "It's past and forgotten."

"I'll find a way of making it all up to you someday. I have a lot of ground to cover, starting from the moment you found Jeff's body until a few months ago."

She smiled through her tears. "I hope you're aware that could take some doing."

"You could sentence me to a life term."

"Consider yourself sentenced." She raised her arms and Jordan wrapped her in his embrace. He buried his face in her neck and drank in her love.

"You never tried to contact me," she whispered, "not even once."

"When?"

"These past few months. I needed you the most then."

"But you said you didn't want to see me!" He'd never understand a woman's mind. Staying away had been torment, but he'd had no choice but to abide by her wishes. Now she was telling him she'd wanted him.

"You won't have to worry about that happening again," he assured her. "I've got a life sentence and I'm not about to be cheated out of a single day."

Molly smiled softly and directed his mouth to hers. "The penalty should start soon, don't you think?"

Jordan laughed and then his lips met hers. He wondered if a single lifetime was enough time for him to properly love this woman.

* * * * *

IT'S OUR 1000TH SILHOUETTE ROMANCE, AND WE'RE CELEBRATING!

JOIN US FOR A SPECIAL COLLECTION OF LOVE STORIES BY AUTHORS YOU'VE LOVED FOR YEARS, AND NEW FAVORITES YOU'VE JUST DISCOVERED. JOIN THE CELEBRATION...

April
REGAN'S PRIDE by Diana Palmer
MARRY ME AGAIN by Suzanne Carey

May
THE BEST IS YET TO BE by Tracy Sinclair
CAUTION: BABY AHEAD by Marie Ferrarella

June
THE BACHELOR PRINCE by Debbie Macomber
A ROGUE'S HEART by Laurie Paige

July
IMPROMPTU BRIDE by Annette Broadrick
THE FORGOTTEN HUSBAND by Elizabeth August

SILHOUETTE ROMANCE...VIBRANT, FUN AND EMOTIONALLY RICH! TAKE ANOTHER LOOK AT US! AND AS PART OF THE CELEBRATION, READERS CAN RECEIVE A FREE GIFT!

YOU'LL FALL IN LOVE ALL OVER
AGAIN WITH
SILHOUETTE ROMANCE!

Silhouette®
TM

CEL1000

**Rugged and lean...and the best-looking,
sweetest-talking men to be found in the
entire Lone Star state!**

_Diana
Palmer_

LONG, TALL
TEXANS

In July 1994, Silhouette is very proud to bring you
Diana Palmer's first three LONG, TALL TEXANS.
CALHOUN, JUSTIN and TYLER—the three cowboys
who started the legend. Now they're back by popular
demand in one classic volume—and they're ready to
lasso your heart! Beautifully repackaged for this
special event, this collection is sure to be a
longtime keepsake!

"Diana Palmer makes a reader want to find a Texan
of her own to love!"   —*Affaire de Coeur*

**LONG, TALL TEXANS—the first three—
reunited in this special roundup!**

**Available in July,
wherever Silhouette books are sold.**

Montana Mavericks™

Stories that capture living and loving beneath the Big Sky, where legends live on...and the mystery is just beginning.

Watch for the sizzling debut of MONTANA MAVERICKS in August with

ROGUE STALLION

by Diana Palmer

A powerful tale of simmering desire and mystery!

And don't miss a minute of the loving as the mystery continues with:

THE WIDOW AND THE RODEO MAN
by Jackie Merritt (September)
SLEEPING WITH THE ENEMY
by Myrna Temte (October)
THE ONCE AND FUTURE WIFE
by Laurie Paige (November)
THE RANCHER TAKES A WIFE
by Jackie Merritt (December)
and many more of your favorite authors!

Only from **▼ Silhouette®**

where passion lives.

Silhouette

SPECIAL EDITION

™

That

SPECIAL

Woman!

ONE OF OUR OWN
Cheryl Reavis

Getting custody of her orphaned nephew was the hardest thing Sloan Baron had ever faced. She found herself on unfamiliar New Mexico territory, forced to battle stubborn Navaho policeman Lucas Singer. Lucas was as stubborn as Sloan was feisty, but soon she found herself undeniably attracted....

Don't miss ONE OF OUR OWN, by Cheryl Reavis, available in August!

She's friend, wife, mother—she's you! And beside each Special Woman stands a wonderfully *special* man. It's a celebration of our heroines— and the men who become part of their lives.

Don't miss **THAT SPECIAL WOMAN!** each month— from some of your special authors! Only from Silhouette Special Edition!